A HELL TO PAY
NOVELLA

FLAME'S DAWN

JILLIAN DAVID

Crimson Romance

New York London Toronto Sydney New Delhi

CRIMSON
ROMANCE

Crimson Romance
An Imprint of Simon & Schuster, Inc.
1230 Avenue of the Americas
New York, NY 10020

ISBN 978-1-4405-9718-3
ISBN 978-1-4405-9719-0 (ebook)

CHAPTER 1

January 31, 1968, 2 a.m.

Captain Barnaby Blackstone wiped the relentless drip of sweat from his forehead. His CO had sworn that Barnaby would get used to the heat, yet here he stood, three months after deployment, still sweating. In January. Bollocks.

Vietnam. A hell of a place to torture a limey used to fifty-degree weather.

But a hell of a great place for that same limey to pick up plenty of kills.

God's teeth, he so wanted the Meaningful Kill—the one action that might complete his immortal contract. If he could just get back to the battles where the selection of kills was abundant.

Most men would have jumped at the chance to get out of the jungle and away from the fighting. Not Barnaby.

Unfortunately, what he needed wasn't in Saigon. Additional information that might provide the key to escaping his eternal servitude lay buried in the Forbidden City, tucked within the ancient Vietnamese capital city of Hue, 400 miles to the north.

In the current epicenter of hell.

In Hue, where his possible salvation lay, the Vietcong, south Vietnamese, and U.S. troops all converged in an attempt to remove each other from the face of this Earth. Not the best time for him to attempt a wild goose chase for scrolls that might or might not contain the key to breaking the curse that had forced him to commit murders for centuries.

He froze at a scampering noise and stared down a side street, searching for a possible new kill. He spied only a scrawny dog, scavenging in the night. Barnaby could relate.

Criminy, he'd had enough of this disgusting existence as an eternal hit man.

Scratching at the unnaturally short regulation haircut, he cursed as his thick cotton uniform adhered like a warm, wet washcloth to his overheated skin. Man wasn't fit to live in this sauna. Even if that sauna had nice scents of things like yellow apricot flowers and chrysanthemums, abundant in this season of Tet.

Man wasn't meant to kill each other in a hellhole like this, either. Nevertheless, battles and death were happening, as they had happened in many places for centuries. Lord knew, Barnaby had watched history repeat itself far too many times over the years.

So why wasn't he enjoying the hiatus from hell during Tet, the Vietnamese New Year? This traditional holiday marked a break in the fighting, when all the North Vietnamese took naps, drank *bai hoi*, and sang songs to Uncle Ho. Why was he trudging back through the shadowy, humid Saigon streets at this godforsaken hour?

Because the communications system had lit up like a Christmas tree seven hours ago, right as he ended his shift, and then his sixth sense had the bad manners to drag his arse out of bed at hell knows what hour. God's teeth, every city and town in the entire bloody country had simultaneously gone to shite.

Barnaby flinched at another pulse of mental warning. His preternatural instincts had gone plumb off the charts, with all needles on the dial pointing directly to the tall rectangular building before him. The U.S. embassy's exoskeleton, like shadowy honeycombs, covered all but the first floor of the building. The outer wall, with its concrete waffle squares lined up side by side to create a ten-foot-high barrier around the building, protected the exposed windows of the embassy's first floor.

Solid. Guarded. Safest place in all of Vietnam.

So why did his sixth sense urge him to return here tonight?

Flashing his credentials, he passed through the main gate and then between two Marine MPs at the side door. He yanked the warm metal handle and tapped his shiny shoes down a linoleum floor and into a marginally cooler office.

Inside, the rhythmic drone of the anemic fan did little to improve the sweltering evening air.

Unlike the aqua-blue eyes staring back at him from a desk near the back of the large office. Cool, clear, her gaze felt like swimming in a refreshing ocean. He paused, half expecting to hear waves and seagulls. The temperature on his warm brow dropped ten degrees.

His libido cranked up the heat elsewhere.

Communications specialist Jane Larsen had recently transferred to the U.S. Embassy, after getting ejected from Satan's arse, Khe Sanh. Right after that first horrible attack, the army had yanked her the hell out of there. Since then, Khe Sanh had been blasted halfway to perdition. God's teeth, what was any woman, much less this lovely, soft-spoken angel, doing up near the DMZ?

Rumor had it, she'd volunteered for communications duty up there. Had to be more to the story. The army didn't station women that close to the fighting unless there was a damned good reason. Maybe that reason had to do with the little steno book of Vietnamese and English scribbles that stayed at her side. When she wasn't relaying communications data, she kept the headphones on, bent her head, and jotted down notes in the book.

The CIA's intelligence boys had dropped in far too frequently since she'd arrived at the embassy. Maybe the intel guys' interest had little to do with reports about Charlie's movements and more to do with their need to get their foot in the door with a certain pretty specialist. A growl formed in Barnaby's chest. Those bastards had better keep their interests professional where Jane was concerned.

Or what? She was free to make her own choices. Barnaby had nothing to offer her other than a good tupping. A sweet woman like Jane deserved much more.

She rolled her full lips inward and squirmed.

Fie, he'd been caught staring.

Who wouldn't get caught? From her warm brown hair with swirls of dark honey twisted into a regulation knot at the nape of her elegant neck to her curves cruelly contained by the standard green skirt and off-white blouse, she drew his eye to the point of distraction.

He cleared his throat and aimed for a tone between casual and flirtatious. "So, are you enjoying the music?" They'd discovered a mutual love for modern music a few days ago, and he'd talk music as long as she wanted, if it kept her focus on him.

The horns and soaring tones of Jackie Wilson's "Higher and Higher" came from a dull transistor radio on the major's vacant desk—the desk that sat below a large ground-level window. Verily, Barnaby hated that Jane was stationed in this office. She should be deep in the building in a barricaded room.

Only because of the need to safeguard equipment. Nothing more.

"I suppose." She lay down the headphones she'd removed when he entered the room.

Last woman standing, as it were. At this late hour, all of the day shift had long since gone home, but Jane had stayed behind even though the main center of operations at nearby Tan Son Nhut Air Base took over nighttime communications duties.

"Too quiet, but not quiet enough," she added. What did that mean?

You could hear a pin drop in this office right now.

The scratchy voice in the back of his head fairly screamed at him to get her out of here.

Pulling rank didn't work. She had rebuffed his urgings to go to the women's barracks earlier in the evening. No reason she'd suddenly change her mind.

"How's your evening?" he asked.

If the good feelings generated by that little scrunch of her nose were worth money, maybe he could buy his way out of his damned Indebted contract.

"Sir," she said, tapping a finger on the communications equipment. Her voice flowed like fresh mountain water over his heated skin. "Why did you come back?"

He loved her American accent. *Midwestern* they called it. The words her pink lips formed felt round and open. He could listen to her talk for hours. Preferably with her mouth close to his ear.

"Sir?" she asked again.

"Thought I left something here."

"And you couldn't wait until morning?" The raised chestnut eyebrow indicted him.

"Well, it was—" He rubbed his trimmed hair. "Why are you still here?"

She shook her head. "Not sure. Chatter." Frowning, she said, "I'm worried that something is coming."

"Here?"

"No, Tan Son Nhut." She sighed. "Well, yes, everywhere, actually."

"Really? Have you told anyone?"

"I submitted several reports over the past few days, but I'm not officially an intelligence officer, so my guesses aren't valid."

"But the major has you working here," he waved his hand around the room, "where the sensitive mail and documents are screened."

"I'm here for his communications convenience. Nothing more." A flicker came and went over her shifting ocean-blue eyes.

"So you're just here to do ... what?"

"I can't disc—"

A flash and a percussion shook the building.

Jane yelped and ducked, and Barnaby flew over to hover near her shoulder, shielding her from line of sight of the main office window behind her.

Screams and shouts filtered through the building.

Tapping gunshots and more explosions rattled the window casing.

As lines lit up and buzzed, Jane worked the equipment at a frantic pace. When she peered up at him over her shoulder, that wide-eyed stare rocked him back on his heels as much as the hard blasts right outside the room they were in.

Bloody hell, the world had become a cyclone, and Jane sat firmly in the eye.

Heavy footsteps crescendoed until they abruptly stopped at the doorway. Barnaby snapped a salute to the general.

The older man had aged years in the past few months, deeper lines now bracketing his narrowed eyes. "Screw formality, Blackstone. VC are attacking."

"Sir?" Barnaby asked.

"So you two get the hell out of here."

Jane shifted in the chair. "But what about the troops on the ground? And Tan Son Nhut? They're taking fire. I can't leave my post." She bit her full lower lip and stared at the phones on her desk. "If Tan Son's communications get hit, then the local troops won't be able to report positions and receive orders. And we won't get other ... information."

"Larson, the embassy is breached. VC are pouring into this compound. Screw Tan Son; they have troops there to protect them. Get to the bunker in the basement. Now. That's an order, you two."

"Yes sir," she and Barnaby chorused as the general rushed off.

Thick air buzzed with the rhythm of the off-balance fan punctuated by gunfire and more shouts, louder now.

Wouldn't surprise him if Satan himself rode up the steps of the embassy. Knowing Barnaby's luck, that could literally happen. He chanced a glance around the room and sniffed for brimstone. Nothing more than the humid air that made a man earn each breath.

"Come on. We're going to the basement," he said.

"No, I want—" The communications station crackled to life. She held up her hand and turned a knob while he gritted his teeth. Snapping out coded instructions in English and then switching to Vietnamese, she sent information with a calm confidence that Barnaby had come to crave. She paused to jot down data in the steno pad, then flipped a knob and gave out more terse information.

After she finished, Jane pinned him with a determined expression that made him want to both salute her and wind his arms around her. "I can't leave."

"I don't care. You have to get out of here." He stopped short of grabbing her arm and pulling her bodily out of the room.

"What about the troops who need information? Don't you have friends fighting?"

"Yes. But they can take care of themselves, trust me." He cringed. "Uh, they're pretty tough."

Another explosion went off, this time louder. Z'wounds, he had to get her out of this place.

Paling, she glanced at the ceiling light fixture as it swayed. "The guys out there. That's why I have to stay." She wiped the sheen off her forehead. A whump of helicopter blades increased until it drowned out the shouts in the street and louder bursts of gunfire.

Shite, how he wanted to kiss those quivering lips.

Now was not the time to woolgather. He needed to keep this woman safe, despite herself. What kind of woman served in Vietnam in the first place, much less volunteered to stay at her post and risk death?

A woman with fire in her belly and some kind of mission to accomplish, damn it.

During a lull in the noise, her quiet voice filtered over him, like lace brushing against his ear. He stifled a shudder.

"Aren't you worried?" she asked.

No. Because I cannot die.

"I've got nothing to worry about," he said.

She homed in on him with her teal stare. "You didn't answer my question."

"You're feeling cheeky, then?" Unable to resist inciting a quirk of her eyebrow, he smiled.

"Sorry, but I'm not able to make jokes at a time like this." She swiveled around and went back to work.

Shame settled like a plastic sheet over his warm, damp skin.

The street noise, engine noise, and blades increased in volume. Gunfire erupted, louder now. The shouts of—whom? VC, U.S. troops, South Vietnamese?—filtered through the window.

The warning instinct flared. Faster than an eye blink, he shifted as the window behind her head shattered. He flinched as the bullet winged him and plugged the plaster wall. Damn, it hurt, but if he waited a few minutes, he'd be right as rain.

He'd trade a gunshot wound for the chance to wrap his arms around Jane's soft frame any day.

"Oh my God," she whispered, squeezing his forearm as he snaked it around her upper chest.

He tightened his arm, keeping his torso between hers and the window behind him. A rush of warmth followed by a burning hunger to protect her upended his equilibrium and fogged his brain. When had he last felt so strongly about anyone else? God's wounds, not since Bess. How in heaven's name could a wound fester for hundreds of years?

How could the simple act of holding Jane soothe those same wounds?

With one last squeeze, he groaned as he pushed her out of her chair so she knelt on the floor with the chair partially obscuring her from the window. He pulled his sidearm and crouched down as well, but Barnaby plus a chair offered scant cover from a determined VC with a rifle.

When she turned around, her ocean-blue eyes filled her paper-white face. She darted a glance at his arm.

"You're hit! You need a medic."

"It's nothing."

"Let's get out of here."

He grinned. "Now that's the best idea you've had all evening."

Damn it, the light still swung in the room, illuminating their position for anyone outside the window to see. Barnaby slid with her in front of him toward the door, far enough to reach up and click off the light. Then he scooted her back under the desk while he gathered his wits. His heart pounded. Unusual, considering he didn't fear for his life.

But he feared for Jane's.

Basement. Get to the basement.

Duckwalking and shielding her while additional pops of gunfire impacted the wall behind them, they reached the doorway to the office.

As they scrambled awkwardly out of the office, a door at the end of the hallway burst open. Vietnamese shouts filled the air. Then English words poured from the other end.

And gunfire filled the center of the hall. Right where they crouched.

Hallway. Escape. Not going to work.

Barnaby yanked her back into the dark office and looked around. The window? No. Shots and yells came from the other side of the shattered glass.

They'd have to wait this one out.

If they were lucky.

Bloody hell, he would keep Jane safe or die trying.

The supply closet. Might work.

"Come on," he whispered, holstering the gun as he pulled her along.

Already the wound on his arm had stopped dripping blood. Pain still pummeled him like a pugilist's blows, but at least he could tolerate the discomfort now.

They half crawled, half ran across the room and dove into the office supply closet.

Barnaby shut the door and scrabbled around, working blind in the scant light from the hallway and outside the window that filtered under the closet door. There, he found a mail bag.

He frigging hoped this idea worked.

"Get in here."

"Get in where?" she whispered.

"In this bag. I'm going to tie up the top and tuck you behind the rack, in the corner."

"What?"

"Trust me, Jane. You'll be safe."

After a gut-wrenching delay where she didn't move for a full five seconds, she replied. "Okay."

She blindly patted his arm and worked her way down to his wrist, where he held the bag open. Her soft hands on his skin ignited parts of his body that had been long neglected, and he bit back a curse.

He refused to think of anything besides her safety.

A mere shadow in the darkness, she stepped into the empty canvas bag and crouched down. Her leather pumps brushing over his hand made his groin tighten.

Voices and footsteps traveled down the hall. *Stop thinking about your libido and concentrate on keeping Jane alive.*

Footsteps. Louder. Damn.

The unbalanced fan continued to whir, its ineffective blades seeming to murmur for him to go faster.

More gunshots. The entire canvas bag jumped as he cinched the drawstrings over her head.

"You have to hold still, Jane. Even if someone comes in here, whatever you do, hold still," he whispered.

A muffled response served as assent.

The steps slowed.

Barnaby shoved her into the corner, crammed between the back wall and the end of a metal shelf.

Opening another canvas bag, he stepped into it.

Damnation, letters filled the bottom third of the bag.

The fan whirred. The strains of Herman's Hermits' "There's a Kind of Hush All Over the World" straggled into the closet.

The office light clicked on, pale yellow illumination sliding beneath the closet door.

Barnaby sweated as he worked fast to clear that canvas bag and set the mail on a shelf. He couldn't be bothered to make it look like properly stacked postal products. His hasty shelving job would have to do.

Another footstep. Then two.

As quietly as he could, Barnaby clamped his jaw shut against the twinge in his arm as he opened the bag. He stepped in, but his body didn't completely fit.

Bloody hell.

Glass crunched outside the closet door.

Barnaby shoved his six-foot frame down as far into the bag as possible and raised the top of the bag.

When he cinched the top, it stopped just above his brows. His buzzed scalp stuck out.

The doorknob rattled, and Barnaby's heart stopped. He bent toward Jane, hoping to heaven that the top of his head wouldn't be visible in this position.

After a shout in Vietnamese farther away, whoever stood outside the closet replied with foreign words.

The metal door creaked on worn hinges. Barnaby froze.

He was so close to her, Barnaby could hear Jane's short, sharp breaths, muffled through the canvas, like she had her hand over her mouth. Her body shook, and he wanted to drag her into his arms and soothe her trembling.

The door swung open, and whoever stood there muttered something in Vietnamese.

One step, then two, closer to their hiding spot. Jane twitched, and Barnaby prayed the person at the door didn't notice.

At another shout from down the hall, the person in the office barked back. Crunching treads faded toward the front lobby.

Another round of gunfire erupted. English shouts and then more footsteps pounding down the hall.

Then silence.

CHAPTER 2

Jane couldn't breathe. The air had turned stale in the thick cloth bag, and her legs shook with the effort to hold her crouched position. Never mind that if the VC caught her, they'd have a treasure trove of secrets the likes of which they'd never imagined. No one, not even the major, knew the extent of her work with the CIA.

Joining the intelligence community had seemed like a good idea four years ago. But how much could a high school student really understand about a foreign country that had only been briefly covered in world history class?

Apparently a lot and about Vietnam in particular, as her indoctrination into the CIA attested. In fact, a high school student gifted in learning languages and pattern recognition could become an operative who could contribute to the intelligence efforts here in Vietnam. However, her training hadn't prepared her for what she'd seen in Khe Sanh. And training sure as heck hadn't prepared her for the real possibility of death or capture.

What about her transfer to a safer location, the embassy?

Safer. What a total joke.

She flinched at a loud rap outside the building. She'd gone from life in a tailspin to being part of a mission with the CIA to crawling out of a mailbag.

Forget about direction and purpose. All she wanted now was to get out of this insane country.

More *rat-a-tats* outside the building rattled her nerves.

And to add insult to injury, that stupid old radio kept on cranking out the American Top 40 hits as if nothing was wrong. As if VC wasn't five steps away from finding and killing her. The upbeat chorus of "Daydream Believer" taunted her on every level. Damn those space cadet Monkees.

Judging by the volume of the shouts and pops of ammunition, fighting continued but on another floor or was being repelled outside. But she and Barnaby weren't out of danger yet.

Movement from the warm body leaning against hers made her jump. The rustling of the canvas seemed way too loud.

Barnaby had done exactly as he'd promised. He'd kept her safe.

Fear and relief crystallized into a stark need for Barnaby's arms to slide around her and hold on tight.

Be careful what you wish for. A date within two mailbags was not exactly what she had in mind.

A tendril of coolness made her gulp in fresh air as Barnaby uncinched the top of the sack and helped her out of the hiding spot. His hands, strong and sure, supported her as she stepped out of the bag.

Behind him, the closet door stood open. In the semidarkness, the office furniture loomed large and menacing, throwing shadows that could hide anything. Or anyone.

Panic clawed at her. She should have listened to the general, should have listened to Barnaby. Should have left Vietnam after Khe Sanh. But no, she'd had this warped sense of duty. If she had no purpose, she had nothing, and her personal safety be damned.

Even now, the communications equipment crackled in the office, daring her to continue doing her job.

Well, forget that.

"Are you all right?" Barnaby's whisper caressed her as surely as if he'd touched her face.

"Yes, thanks to you."

She needed him to continue to hold on to her arm. Needed the tether of his strength to keep from going to pieces. He had become her anchor in this dark closet.

More pops and explosions, quieter now, drifted back to their hiding spot.

"Stay or go?" he asked.

"Pardon?"

"Stay in this closet or try to find safety?"

Shouts that she translated as barked VC commands came from the floor above them. Or was it down the hall? She was too frazzled to think clearly. Tremors shot through her body.

"We don't know what's out there. I'm not even sure where to run to at this point." She cursed how her voice wavered. "But we're sitting ducks in here, if someone came back."

"You are correct."

The warmth in his tone gave her strength, while also making her want to curl up into his muscled frame and hide from the mad world.

"Can we stay here for a while longer?" she asked.

"That's as good a plan as any, milady."

What was the deal with this guy? With her ear for language, she'd noted his accent and word choices slid in and out of normal patterns. This wasn't the first time she'd detected a slight English accent that he tried to hide. Who was Barnaby Blackstone?

The man had saved her life; that's who he was. Maybe he had his own secrets—who didn't?—but bottom line, he had promised to keep her safe and had made good on that promise. It was a solid enough track record for Jane right at that moment.

When he leaned away, her fingers uncurled and splayed out toward him in an unconscious movement. With effort, she pushed her hands down to her sides.

"All right." His low voice, a notch above a whisper, flowed over her. "I'll just pull the door shut. Don't worry. I won't let anyone harm you."

The creak of unoiled hinges set her nerves on edge. Everyone in Southeast Asia could hear the noise.

Once the door closed, she relaxed. Something about Barnaby's confident manner made her believe he would stop a tank to keep her safe.

His form was a mere shadow. Their too-loud breaths punctuated the still air.

"Barnaby, I—thank you."

A pause. In the darkness, his hand returned to her arm, startling her until his thumb brushed circles over her skin. "My pleasure."

The shakes had set in for real now.

"My dear, you're shivering."

"Only nerves, which makes sense." Of course it makes sense. Everything made sense to brave Jane, the girl who in high school found herself with no family, then pulled herself together and became a linguistics and pattern expert for the CIA. Wow. And just look at her now, cowering in a closet.

"Here."

In the darkness, she startled at the rasp as he scooted the burlap sacks under a metal shelf. Then, with gentle, steady hands, he backed her up a step until she sagged against the corner of the closet farthest away from the door. Barnaby's broad chest brushed against her, and she rested a hand near his heart. Each steady thud under her fingertips fortified her nerves. His stance made it obvious: Anyone who wanted to get to her would be going through him first.

The thought both excited and unsettled her.

"May I?" he asked, his low voice rocking her back on her heels.

Man, he was so close to her.

"May you what?"

"Do this." He snaked an arm around the small of her back and another around her shoulders.

When he pulled her close, she gripped his shirt in two fists and held on for dear life.

"Shush, dear. You're safe," he murmured, almost to himself.

He slid his hand into the hair that had come free of her regulation bun. The sensation of his fingers on her scalp sent heavenly shivers down her spine. When he urged her head forward into the crook of his solid chest and shoulder, she nearly came apart by the tenderness of the act.

While he crooned nonsense words, she gave in to her nerves and sagged into his muscled frame, inhaling his light cologne and potent, earthy scent. For just a few moments, maybe she didn't have to go it alone. Maybe she didn't have to put up a brave front and be the first to volunteer for a risky mission. Instead of searching for her purpose, she could take the comfort offered.

Maybe she didn't have to do everything by the book.

They were in a closet. In a foreign country. During a war. And Charlie with guns prowled outside the office, eager to kill them.

Regulations be damned.

It took a few moments to register his lips whispering over her forehead. Firm but soft, his mouth traveled over her hairline, trailing warmth and pleasure.

In the darkness, his hand tightened over her lower back, creating the slightest arch of her body toward his.

And boy, did she like it.

When he made another circuit of her hairline, she turned her face up and intercepted his mouth when he reached her temple.

The brush of his lips against her lower one tilted her equilibrium. At his sharp intake of breath, she froze. Okay, she had crossed a major line. She got it.

"I'm so sor—"

He smothered anything she had to say with a hungry kiss that made her thankful for the wall behind her. So hard did he kiss her, when she gasped, the air she inhaled came from his body, feeding her, sustaining her.

Even as she slid her hands to the nape of his neck and tugged him closer, he needed no encouragement, judging by the growls of male interest rumbling from his chest into her bones. She felt the vibrations all the way down to her toes.

At an explosion in the distance, his arms tensed like iron bands, but he still held her in a gentle embrace.

Jane couldn't change the circumstances of their situation, but at least she could make the best of things while they hid from the VC.

If only his kisses didn't make her want to squeal. The one action that would put both of them in immediate danger.

So she focused on her growing passion instead. She met his mouth, desire matching desire, as she experimented with angles and levels of pressure, testing the limits of his abilities.

Who would've thought? He had no weaknesses in the kissing category. Not a one.

As a matter of fact, he got extra points when he slid his tongue between her lips and took the kiss to a whole new level.

Clutching at his corded shoulders, she hung on as he used his mouth in new and amazing ways. Her breasts tingled and her core ached; he had her so turned on as he transported her to a place a world away from Vietnam.

In a single smooth move, he slid his hand under her blouse. The rasp of his palm skimming over her stomach sent her into orbit and made her strain on her tiptoes to arch into him even more. With feather light passes, he stroked her skin until she tingled with the need to have his hands on every inch of her body.

Their breathing, his low growls, and her little gasps were the only sounds to fill the closet. Nothing else mattered. Nothing else could hurt her as long as Barnaby had her in his arms.

"Oh my dear, you're so sweet, so beautiful," he groaned, rubbing his thumbs over her plain, nylon bra.

When he rolled a nipple between his fingers, she would have collapsed if not for his strong arm anchoring her to his heated torso.

Exactly as it should be.

The thought rocked her to the core. They fit perfectly.

He dipped a hand lower, over her hip, and ran a fingertip under the hem of her skirt.

"Barnaby," she breathed. The hand disappeared, leaving a void that craved his touch. "What's wrong?"

He stroked her hair. "Nothing at all, my dear. I'm just ... you're an amazing woman. I want to ... but I won't if you don't— Just know that I understand if ... Criminy." He groaned and rested his chin on the top of her head.

"Don't stop on my behalf." No more coloring between the lines. They only had right now, and she wanted him, plain and simple.

"Are you sure?"

She groped for his hand in the darkness and hooked it under her skirt.

"Completely certain."

CHAPTER 3

Forget the knife lust, Barnaby's mind had become consumed with another hunger altogether. The ever-present need to kill had been surmounted by his need for Jane. Not since 1553 had he wanted a woman so badly.

Not any woman, but Jane, this woman with a fierce commitment to her job despite personal danger, a sweet smile that greeted him every morning, and a body that seemed designed to nestle perfectly against his own.

Speaking of which, when she gave that breathy sigh against his mouth, the perfection of the sound sent a jolt of desire into his hard cock.

He slid his fingers inward along the skirt fabric. The heat between her legs felt like the sweetest, most perfect warmth, and he inched his fingers upward. Her delicate floral scent, like those yellow apricot flowers here in Saigon, surrounded him.

God's teeth, what he'd give to see her treasures for himself! But without light, his other senses became amplified, as if his mind wanted to imprint the memory of her into his soul. Every sound she made set his nerves on edge. Every sweep of his rough palm over her silky skin elicited an answering tightness in his groin. The tiny noises she held back as they both tried to remain unheard ... he wanted to be inside of her posthaste.

When she gripped his arm where the bullet had passed through, he couldn't reconcile the mixture of pain from his rapidly healing wound and the pleasure of her hands on his body. He wanted more of her contradictions—pleasure with pain, sweet but seductive, soft and tough. Her invasion of his senses threatened to render him senseless. He had to have more of her.

Hooking her undergarment with a finger, he slowly drew the lightweight fabric down her legs until she stepped out of it.

The wondrous world of her flesh and her pleasure was his to explore. Verily, he wanted to feast upon her, take his time, draw out her passion. But whatever might occur outside the door necessitated a more time-sensitive encounter tonight.

As he brushed a finger over her core, he absorbed the surprised gasp with his mouth. She was eager for him if her pelvis rocking against his hand was any indication.

Leaning back to unzip his pants, he thanked the holy host that modern garments had much faster access for times like this.

He couldn't see it, but his cock, hard and ready, pointed toward Jane. Obviously, it knew what it wanted.

He leaned into her, his damp tip brushing over her soft flesh before it stopped at her closed thighs. She shifted and bumped against the wall.

With the close quarters, he needed a creative solution to this untenable conundrum. Patting over the shelving in the closet, he found a solid metal level that would do brilliantly.

"Lift your leg a bit," he whispered.

She nipped and licked his lip, making him forget his name. Then she complied, and he directed her foot and trim ankle to a shelf a few feet off the ground.

Another stroke of her soft flesh, and she trembled enough to rattle the shelving. He separated her folds and nudged the head of his cock into her slick core.

Pressing her bent leg outward, he swiveled her hips to accept more of his shaft. Heaven and hell shot through his body at the contact, and he wanted to drive into her, mark her as his own, and fill her completely. With brute force of willpower, he held his Indebted strength in check. Barely.

With slow, looping movements, he stroked until she gloved him. As he kissed her again, he pushed the rhythm faster, picking her off the ground with each thrust and swallowing her moans of pleasure.

When he nudged her leg open further, the bliss of seating himself so impossibly deep inside pushed him to the edge. The skirt material bunched at her waist; he shoved the bra up over her breasts. Barnaby wanted to contact all of her, all at once.

As her faint cries hit that perfect high pitch of the calm before the storm, he slowed down. Oh, sweet torture! She could torment him like this until the end of time, with nary a complaint from him.

Unable to resist, he sped up and thrust faster than was humanly possible, driving her beyond normal human response, pushing his pleasure beyond anything he'd experienced before.

With a death grip on his shoulders, she clutched at him and released with a hoarse gasp that she bit off. Beautiful spasms held him a willing prisoner inside of her body, and he followed a few seconds later, pouring out his release inside of her core. He wanted to fill her with himself, wanted to brand her ... as his own?

Cold fear clutched at his chest as he struggled to reconcile his mind: two halves of an ill-fitting whole. What future did he have with this fierce and sexy woman in his arms? Did he really want to number her in his various tuppings over the centuries? He had nothing to give any woman besides a romp in the sheets.

As a matter of fact, had Jane known about Barnaby's true disgusting nature as a cursed Indebted killer, she might have preferred to take her chances with the VC.

With reluctance and guilt, he eased out of her and kissed the salt from her brow. He wrapped his arms around her trembling frame as his mind spun.

What a pickle. He couldn't play fast and loose with her emotions in this stressful situation. Yet, that's exactly what he was doing, wasn't it?

All he could offer her was this sweaty, quick slaking of their mutual need in a dark closet. Unacceptable. Not enough for a woman like Jane.

Not for the first time in more than 400 years, he felt inadequate and unworthy as a man.

He helped her back into her undergarment and smoothed her skirt down. Tucking her into his arms again, he rested his chin on her silky hair and fought back his shame.

Unworthy as a man? Laughable.

He was no man. He was an ungodly scourge upon this world.

Barnaby, the wretched creation of Satan, was the thing nightmares were made of.

• • •

It had taken all of Jane's focus to keep from crying out at the delicious release in Barnaby's arms. She had no idea that he had such strength, but when he held her as he drove deep inside, she craved more of the power in his arms, in his muscled frame, in his protective spirit.

He pulled away to readjust his clothing, and she did the same. In an unconscious move, she caught herself leaning toward him. He was her anchor in a sea of insanity that swirled around her.

And now, he drifted away from her. Fitting, since The 5th Dimension belted out "Up, Up and Away" on the radio, in all their flute-punctuated oblivion to the ridiculous circumstances here in the altered reality of Vietnam.

Barnaby? Oh, he remained physically close, even dropping light kisses on her forehead once more and draping his arms around her. But the intimacy she longed for? Gone, like a curtain had fallen between them.

As she should have expected. Men in the service here didn't want a forever kind of girl, and tonight's bad decision proved that point.

If only her soul didn't crave more of him.

If only he didn't seem to fit her in every way possible.

Had to be the stress of war. No woman would be fool enough to believe that forever could come from stolen moments in a closet, hiding from the enemy.

So just like that, while she reeled from the amazing sex, Jane shoved the pieces of herself back together again.

Footsteps traveled down the hall outside the office, and she tensed. Barnaby put a hand up on the metal shelf, shielding her with his big frame.

She tugged at her wrinkled clothing.

The door flew open, and light speared her eyes.

"Larson, are you in there?"

Peeking out from under Barnaby's arm, she spied the general's furrowed brow. The air left her in a big whoosh, and she sagged against the wall.

"Yes sir."

"What ... are you doing in there?" he asked.

"Hiding from Charlie, sir," Barnaby growled, still staring at Jane. With the closet light streaming in from above and behind him, she still couldn't make out his expression.

After a full five seconds, he relaxed his rigid posture and held a steady hand out to her. When she took it, Barnaby guided her over the canvas bags and out of the closet. He briefly explained to the general how they had evaded the VC.

The older man rubbed his jowls. "I'm glad you two are safe. When I didn't see you in the bunker downstairs, I worried that both of you ..."

"Barnaby's quick thinking saved us," she said, trying to smooth her hair into a semblance of regulation appropriate.

Chopper blades split the air in the distance. Pops of gunfire outside made her flinch.

"What happened?" Barnaby asked.

"VC breached the building. The marines finally flushed the VC out, sealed the breach, and swept the premises, but it wasn't without casualties." He grimaced.

Men died defending the embassy while Jane had enjoyed a quickie with Barnaby. Guilt tasted sour on her tongue.

The general stared at her above the rims of his glasses, his tired eyes drooping. "You're out of here, Larson."

"Pardon, sir?"

"You're leaving on the next transport." He pointed upward.

"But I have to—"

"Intel says these attacks are going to get worse before they get better. Any nonessentials—"

"Nonessentials?"

"Okay, not really in your situation, but I refuse to put a woman in the line of fire. The world's gone mad out there, Larson, and I don't care how good you are at your job. I will not have your blood on my hands."

"Thanks," she bit out. Nothing like boiling down her value into a way to prevent someone's feelings of guilt.

He crossed his arms. "Other women and also children of staff are getting evac'ed tonight. You do good work, Larson, and we're going to miss that. But these orders come from your ... superiors."

When she opened her mouth one more time, Barnaby cut her off. "I can't agree more, sir. Where does she need to go?"

What? Barnaby wanted her to leave, too?

"To the roof," the general barked. The hum of the chopper had gotten louder. "Now."

"Roger," Barnaby said.

"Sir?" Jane asked his retreating back.

He spun on a heel. "You'll have a letter of recommendation from me when you get back stateside. I'll see to it." He waved his hand. "Go on, now. I have work to do here."

Nothing felt quite so awkward as the uncomfortable silence that filled the room. What could she do? There was no arguing with the general this time.

"So, we'd better ..." she said.

Barnaby gave a brief nod. "Right."

After she collected a few things from the desk, he guided her up the stairs and onto the roof, where several American and South Vietnamese women and their family members stood.

On the horizon, soft flashes of light flickered in the night sky, followed a few seconds later by poofs of sound that made her shiver, despite the thick, humid air. Off in the distance, bursts of tapping echoed back to where she stood.

In a minute, she was going to leave all of this. For what? Would they call her back in-country after the fighting ended? Would she be relegated to the typing pool? Or worse, would she be discharged from the only work that had given her empty life a purpose?

More importantly, what about Barnaby?

Even now, he assumed a stance that partially blocked her from the debris blowing from the landing helicopter. Still protecting her.

As the soldier in the copter yelled for her to get aboard, she looked up at Barnaby. The stark pain on his face squeezed her heart.

"I want to see you again." His shout cut through the rotor noise.

"What?"

"I'll find you."

"If you say so."

"I say so. Tell me where."

Only a few steps away from the landing skid on the helicopter, she jerked toward him when he caught her by the upper arm. He kissed her until her head swam.

Cupping her face in his hands, he stared at her, as though to memorize her face. "Do you trust me?"

The question took her aback. She had no reason not to trust him, as a matter of fact.

He brushed her hair back. "Where should I look?" he asked next to her ear.

If she didn't get reassigned, she'd go to the closest thing she had to a home. "San Francisco." No way could he find her there. And no time to give detailed instructions.

His eyes had gone jet black, probably a trick of the shadows. "I will find you." The intensity in his promise made her shiver.

Then he boosted her into the aircraft and stepped back, a blank expression on his handsome face.

I'll find you.

A nice sentiment.

As the helicopter lifted off, an odd whistle caught her attention, right before an explosion obliterated the rooftop.

Waves of sound and light shoved the helicopter into a sick pendulum, threatening to dump her out of the open side door, until the pilot righted the vehicle and pushed the helicopter higher.

She searched the burning rooftop.

Barnaby?

Between flames and smoke, dark shapes littered the rooftop, some writhing, others still.

Barnaby?

Squinting in the smoky air, she scanned the carnage.

A body lay, unmoving, right where Barnaby had stood.

Chapter 4

San Francisco, April 1974

The smooth organ and guitar of Santana's "Evil Ways" escaped from a beat-up radio propped outside a run-down café on Haight Street. Barnaby grimaced at the lyrics as he hurried past row after row of distressed properties.

Everything about this area pulled him down—the sagging porches, boarded windows, and burned out hippies begging on corners. He understood poverty. But this area didn't bother him because of the sad remnants of the Summer of Love from several years ago. He didn't even mind the wrecked buildings.

The entire area reeked of sadness. Even the spring sunshine got tangled up in the clouds overhead.

Maybe that oppressive sense of hopelessness was why he kept coming back here. This place hid criminals. Criminy, his knife loved the opportunities to obtain a kill. Barnaby had to feed those Indebted urges. Even better, criminals had come to this area to disappear from the world. His soul blade was only too happy to oblige.

What Barnaby hadn't obliged was his promise to search for Jane. Oddly, no one in the military seemed to know her whereabouts. All records of Jane stopped right after she returned to the United States.

So just like that, he'd given up, hadn't he?

Instead of looking for her, he had spent the last however many years biding his time until he could return safely to Vietnam and continue his search for those damned scrolls. Just because Indebted were difficult to kill didn't mean he could saunter into enemy territory and expect to survive. So he waited.

In the meantime, he slogged through the monotony of his existence: finding and killing corrupt souls, punctuated by the occasional tupping of a willing woman when the mood struck him. And when a specific mood struck, he drowned his recollection of one particular night with a certain woman in a certain closet with as much drink as possible. Anything to keep those haunting memories at bay.

So basically, nothing. He had nothing to show for the past six years.

Or the past 400, for that matter.

Adjusting his polyester vest over the stretchy paisley shirt, he squirmed. Whatever happened to wool, linen, and quilted material? Gone, along with doublets and codpieces. Only space-age fabrics like polyester, whatever sorcery that was, would do for this brave new world.

Speaking of the space age, he raised an eyebrow as a couple walked by. Both man and woman wore nothing but vinyl and aluminum foil and big, loose grins. The cloud of thick, sweet smoke they exhaled put Barnaby in the mood for a snack.

A movement out of the corner of his eye stopped him dead in his tracks.

That little sensation, his odd little extra instinct that he'd learned to trust over the years, caught his attention. Why? It wasn't his Indebted urges driving him, but his sixth sense. It kept him one step ahead of danger, and he'd had the ability long before becoming Indebted.

Unfortunately, the instinct wasn't specific. It didn't provide directions. It didn't solve anything. The itchy-scalp sensation only meant he should pay close attention.

But to what?

To whom?

He leaned against the solid brick of a storefront and scanned 180 degrees, trying to find anything that seemed unusual.

In this area of town, though, everything felt wrong.

Spying another flicker within a cracked window, Barnaby halted his perusal and studied the spot. Could be squatters. Could be anything. Dusting his hands on his flared jeans, he took a few steps toward the building.

A police cruiser pulled up, black, rectangular, and staffed with two no-nonsense officers with twin scowls. They had that look of men searching for anything out of place.

Out of place defined Barnaby. Out of time, too. As good as his counterfeit IDs might be, he never wanted to push his luck. Best to remain inconspicuous. Ignoring his sixth sense, he shifted to his left and strolled away to the east, back to his studio apartment several miles away in the Tenderloin District.

An Indebted like Barnaby didn't care that he lived in the worst neighborhood of San Francisco. He was nearly indestructible and stronger than any mortal.

Nowadays, there wasn't much that scared him.

• • •

Jane's world tilted sideways as she clung to the grimy toilet and barfed the booze and Quaaludes out of her burning stomach. She'd taken them dutifully, but as soon as the opportunity presented itself, she lurched to the bathroom, hoping, praying, she could get them out of her system fast enough. She didn't know how many more drug trips she could handle here at the San Francisco branch of the People's Palace.

If she never heard the late Jimi Hendrix's screaming metal acid trip song, "Machine Gun" again, it would be too soon. But in the People's Palace, Hendrix's postmortem magnum opus had become the national anthem of Nutsville, California.

At least someone had changed the album. Now "Hooked on a Feeling" by Blue Swede tormented her, along with the ridiculous "ooga chocka" lyrics that fit perfectly with her retching pattern.

God, if she had thought her exit from Vietnam and entry into the newly created Drug Enforcement Agency indicated an upwardly mobile career, the vile mixture of pills, alcohol, and bile swirling into the grungy porcelain abyss told another tale. Joining the DEA had seemed like a good idea at the time. Now, alone and undercover with nonexistent support, her career teetered on the edge of oblivion.

Her supervisor had warned her that the suits were about to yank her ass out of this operation if she couldn't produce the goods, but Jane smelled something fishy. Why would the DEA send their most inexperienced operative into a well-known cult where the stakes were sky high only to have her fail? It made no sense. Unless someone at the DEA wanted her to fail.

Damn it, time was running out. She had to get more information and fast. But how?

Nausea returned in another vicious wave, and she focused on ejecting the rest of the drugs into the bowl.

She wouldn't get more intel by drinking Alice's potion or eating Alice's damned cake. And this sure as hell wasn't Wonderland.

As her stomach settled, Jane took a big breath.

When she stood, the world spun again. Oh man, despite her attempts to get rid of the drugs, they'd still hit her brain. She'd waited too long. Damn it, she needed to veg out for a few minutes.

In an effort to clear her foggy vision, she turned the dull sink handle and splashed tepid water on her face. Anything to sober up. Blinking hard, she managed to restore her equilibrium enough to remain upright and concentrate on the world around her. The image looking back at her in the mirror made her want to throw up again. With bloodshot eyes and long, stringy hair, she'd transformed into the perfect junkie.

Talk about lack of credibility.

With a few deep breaths to clear her head, she took time to wait for her fellow adherents to pass out. They'd all consumed

God-knows-what drugs during the rousing conclusion to the "homily" delivered by loony tunes cult leader Tim Thompson.

Good news and bad news: Thompson had taken a liking to her. If only she could fend off his propositions long enough to get concrete intel on his organization. She walked a tightrope, suspended hundreds of feet in midair, trying to get close—but not too close—to the disgusting leader. But she had a mission to accomplish, and she would succeed, damn it.

Minutes later, when she cracked the bathroom door, the main sounds were of some hallucinating couples making sloppy love. Other noises of light breathing and snores drifted back to her. Shadows shifted as lava climbed lamps. But no other movement. Good.

Easing into the hall, she stepped carefully, rolling her bare feet as she'd been taught in the DEA's too-brief training. Truth be told, those uptight Washington suits had no idea what to do with women in their cadre, much less how to run an undercover drug trafficking investigation where morality was painted in shades of gray.

And being a woman? The DEA folks taught women grudgingly at best. So she'd done this assignment as on-the-job training.

What the DEA wanted was a mole who could keep herself alive and deliver enough info for the DEA to make a high-profile bust. Anything to justify its existence as a new government organization.

However, no one realized that this particular mole had infiltrated an outfit a million times more dangerous than anyone had ever guessed. Drugs only scratched the surface of the goings on in the People's Palace.

Even more concerning, someone in the DEA might have a finger in the pot, so to speak.

Clowns to the left of me, jokers to the right, as the Stealers Wheel would say.

She lifted her foot over a tangle of two sets of feet and continued down the hall toward the front door of the run-down painted lady house. At a creak in the old wood floor, she froze. She fought back a flashback of rusty hinges squeaking in the humid air of Saigon.

For a split second, she could feel Barnaby's heated frame pressed against her body. She shivered at the memory of his hands on her skin and their desperate kisses in the dark.

But that had been a world away and a different Jane than the mildly intoxicated woman standing in the body-strewn madhouse. Her breath caught on a sob. She'd have given anything to have Barnaby's strong arms around her right about now. What a joke. That fantasy had been blown to bits on that roof in Saigon.

Pulling herself together, she tiptoed out the front door of the cult base and then hurried to a pay phone, two blocks away. She dialed the collect number and gave her security code.

"Larson?" the male voice barked on the other end of the line.

"Yeah." At least the walk had worked the remnants of the 'ludes out of her system. She wasn't nearly as zoned out now.

"Report." Her boss, Howard, had it in for her from day one and never spared more words than necessary on Jane.

Gulping, she plowed ahead. "I don't know how much longer my cover will hold, sir."

"Christ almighty, you're not going to cry on me, are you, Larson?"

She totally wanted to tell this moron where to shove it. Instead, she sucked in a big drag of air and clamped down on her fried nerves. "No. But I'm close to getting solid information about the drug trafficking. Thompson's got ties to several cartels, who are bringing in tons of product to distribute here."

"Good." His voice got quieter, like he was about to hang up.

He couldn't do that. This was her only link to the real world. The normal world. A world without acid trips and hallucinations.

"There's more, sir."

A pause. "Go on."

"Not only is Thompson making lots of money off the drugs, but he's using the money to fund his ... sex trade."

"What?" Her boss must have the phone pressed right up to his face.

"The money goes to purchase women. Some for Thompson, some for other members. Some are sold outside of the organization probably to some politicians, so he makes even more money."

"You have proof?"

"I've heard them talking about it. They have sex houses in other areas of town. I'm close to getting concrete details. It looks like some folks outside of the People's Palace are involved." A sense of ghost fingers closing around her neck distracted her.

"Christ, Larson. After all this time, you still don't know for certain?"

She reeled at the indictment. Not the praise she had expected. "I'm trying, sir. Thompson is starting to notice that I don't participate in some of the more ... intimate activities with group members. I have to try harder to gain his confidence."

"Shit, I knew we shouldn't have sent a women in there. Nicaraguan drug lords? Sex slaves?"

Gritting her teeth, she managed to stay civil. "Pardon, sir?"

"Look, Larson, you're a good girl ..."

Girl? She was twenty-eight. Sure felt like fifty right about now. "But?"

"You're done."

She gripped the phone like she could break it in two. "What?"

"DEA no longer needs your services."

"No longer needs ...?"

An unimpressed grunt came through the phone. "You're done. Go get married and have some kids and a picket fence American dream." His voice had changed. More pressured, less natural.

"Are you seriously firing me, sir?"

"Sorry, Larson. We'll take it from here."

What the hell? "No, I can finish the mission!"

"You're done. The DEA will send you a nice severance package for the service you've done for our country."

"But—"

"Take care now, Larson."

She yelled her objection to the dial tone.

What just happened?

His speech was different than in previous conversations. More tense, the vowels shortened. Choppier. Her language pattern skills took over and analyzed his tight voice. Howard was hiding something.

Nicaraguan drug lords, he'd said.

How did he know about Nicaragua? She had only discovered that connection a few days ago. She hadn't said anything about it to anyone.

The People's Palace was a massive business, and the promise of big bucks could turn anyone.

Even a DEA agent.

As she hurried back up the street to the People's Palace lair, she made her decision. No way would she back down from the mission now. With a little more time, luck, and snooping, she could shut down the People's Palace, help those women, and expose Howard and anyone else involved.

Jane would shove the results of this mission up every one of her lying superiors' asses. She might be low in the pecking order, but she could obtain the info to get them fired.

Actually, she wasn't in the pecking order anymore, was she?

Closing the front door behind her with a tiny click, she froze.

She had two choices: run away and forget that she ever joined the DEA or try for the information that would sink this psychedelic ship of drugs, sex, and government bribery.

Decision made.

She tiptoed around sprawled, sleeping bodies.

Glancing out the partially boarded front window, she spied a man striding up the opposite side of the street. Thick, light brown hair waved off his forehead in a flow that stopped at the nape of his muscled neck. Might not be the regulation cut from Vietnam, but she'd recognize that handsome face anywhere.

Her heart paused. She couldn't breathe.

Barnaby? Alive?

He'd died on that rooftop. She had seen bodies. No one could have survived that explosion.

She rubbed her eyes and looked again. She must be hallucinating. Every cell in her body wanted to find out for certain.

Every cell in her body knew. Him.

Her mission. Her cover. No. She couldn't blow it, not even for him.

A police cruiser slowed down outside of the building, and she ducked away from the window.

"You call the cops?" A rapid clomp of boots and Tim Thompson's harsh voice startled her as she spun around. His second-in-command and smaller, greasier carbon copy, Chuck, hovered at Thompson's shoulder. The two men sported matching grins.

"Wow, you snuck up on me," she said, stalling for time.

Thompson narrowed his snaky eyes and then stared out the window. A flicker of pure evil creased his features as he studied Barnaby's retreating backside. A slow smile twisted his thin lips. He swung his cold gaze back to her. "Where'd you go?"

"Go?" Dude, she couldn't keep her voice calm.

Thompson grabbed her upper arm. "Spill your guts."

"What?"

"You're a cop." So strong was his grip, her hand was going numb.

Her laugh came out too high. "Not a chance." A completely true statement, as of ten minutes ago. "You're in the ozone with ideas like that. You dig?"

His thumb scouring circles on her arm made her wish she'd worn a long-sleeved shirt, and she suppressed a shudder.

When he grinned, no light made it to his soulless stare. "I don't think so." He shifted so the bulge in his tight green Sansabelt slacks couldn't be missed. "You know, I've had my eye on you."

"Oh, well, that's nice." Her attempt at an airy and casual tone failed miserably. Maybe she could still get Barnaby's attention. Out of the corner of her eye, she caught him walking away down the opposite side of the street. No go.

Thompson let go of her arm to push his thinning hair back over his forehead.

Things were going to hell at a rapid rate. The heat in this stifling house made sweat prickle on her scalp. Or was it Thompson's leer that made her sweat?

Her nerves jumped. He stood a few inches away. She had no room to run.

She stepped back and right into Chuck's torso. Damn henchman had blocked her only exit.

Thompson licked his meaty, gross lips. "I'd like to give you a once-in-a-lifetime opportunity, Jane."

"Oh, gosh ..." she managed.

"You're going to be my special companion."

Her heart slammed in her chest. At what point did she think going rogue to complete her doomed DEA mission constituted a good idea? "That's not necessary. I'm fine with how things are now. I'm ... not good enough for you."

With a grin, he drew a cold finger over her cheek.

She flinched but couldn't move, trapped between both men.

Thompson raised his eyebrows. "Things could be so much better, don't you think? Aren't we all on our path to enlightenment?"

"Of course, but—"

"Why would you be here if not to let me ... enlighten ... you?"

Her world tilted again, and it had nothing to do with residual drugs. A path that went in two directions lay before her. Compromise her soul and complete the mission. Compromise her mission and live with the guilt that she'd abandoned those women and let a drug lord slip through her fingers.

Failure was not an option. Not again.

Thompson smiled, his teeth yellow and crooked. "Let's go somewhere more comfortable, shall we?"

She swallowed and gave her best eyelash flutter. "What's in it for me?" Her heart battered against her ribs, a terrified animal trying to get free of its cage.

At that moment, Karen Carpenter's cruel lyrics from "Top of the World" drifted past Jane. Yeah, that Carpenter chick could go blow it out her left nostril.

"I'm in need of a wife to help me maintain peace and harmony around here. As you recall, Linda, my late wife, passed away from a tragic accident a few months ago." His voice sounded off, too sweet and metallic, like the aftertaste from a Tab soda.

And I'm a flying monkey. When not hopped up on drugs, most folks here knew that the circumstances of Thompson's last wife's death were more than suspicious. Did Jane really want to sign up to be next in line?

"How did she help you?" Jane managed.

Chuck snickered.

Thompson rubbed his chin. "Well, she helped me chill when I was strung out. And she managed some business affairs so I had more time to be with my flock."

Slime on top of garbage smelled better than this pile of scum.

But business affairs? That had promise.

If Jane could survive for a little while, she'd have all the intel needed to shut down this organization and maybe take out the mole in the DEA to boot.

Her information could free those poor women being used as sex slaves.

Sacrifice or failure? Which would it be? Didn't look as though she had much of a choice.

Thompson fished out a keychain from his back pocket and nodded toward the stairs. At the top of three flights would be his rooms, his lair.

"Why don't you let me interview you for the position?" He leered.

Those damned Dingo boots preceded her up the stairs and into hell.

CHAPTER 5

San Francisco, July 1974

Barnaby released his hold from a scumbag's collar and let the body slide down the brick wall to crumple on alley pavement. A wave of hope nailed him in the solar plexus as he wiped the cursed blade clean. Was this his Meaningful Kill? An Indebted man could hope.

He didn't normally kill in the daytime, but such a nasty criminal couldn't be missed. This bastard, in the face of his impending death, had blabbed about brokered trades of naive young women in exchange for money or drugs. Good riddance.

At least the knife's lust for corrupt souls had been sated, so one less thing to worry about for a week or so. But no Meaningful Kill. No conclusion to the Indebted contract. Would his boss, Jerahmeel, ever release him?

If Barnaby could get his hands on those damned scrolls, but no, they were hidden in the current most godforsaken place on the planet. He couldn't travel to central Vietnam yet with the war still going on. Maybe soon it would be safer there. Perhaps then he could find a way to stop this macabre merry-go-round his life had become.

Always searching for the next kill.

And criminy, Barnaby couldn't stop returning to the Haight neighborhood.

Had to be some reason for it. He'd stopped doubting his instincts years ago, after he got on the RMS *Titanic* despite the warning bells clanging around in his head.

Four days later, boom, splash. And a lot of treading water and pretending to be hypothermic. On the upside, Barnaby had gotten some good kills for his Indebted quota while waiting for the *Carpathia* to scoop up survivors. So, not a total loss.

Strolling past St. Mary's Hospital, he stopped, riveted, and spun toward the building, like a dowsing rod drawn to water.

Yes sirree, something here. Might not be what he wanted to find, but his sixth sense obviously felt there was something he *needed* to find. Soon.

He stepped into a phone booth and sank a dime into the slot. Squinting at the midday sun, he banked on the fact that his friend, Dante, spent most evenings partying and most days relaxing.

"Yo!" the deep voice blasted through the earpiece.

"Hello, Dante."

"Hi, Barnaby! What's shakin', baby?"

Groaning at his friend's overzealous assimilation of contemporary slang, Barnaby said, "Where are you?"

"San Diego. Sun and babes galore. It's a real love-in. Pretty groovy."

"Got some free time to help me with a project?"

"I'm intrigued. Sure, bro. I was getting bored with the same old lately."

"Ever wanted to work in the medical field?"

"Like a doctor? Can I be a gynecologist?"

Barnaby sputtered. "No. Absolutely not. I was thinking more like you should be an orderly."

"As in I'm a neat, tidy person?"

"No. You get a job as an orderly. Cleaning vomit and giving sponge baths."

"Only if I can totally work on the women's ward."

Barnaby palmed his forehead.

Whatever made Dante happy. Barnaby needed help. "I'm banking on it."

"Count me in, my man! When do you need me to start?"

"Tomorrow. Think you can pull off an infiltration of a hospital? The place is full of nuns."

"Like that's a challenge? I can make any woman's toes curl. Even a shriveled sister!" His laugh rattled the phone. "Seriously, why do you need me to do this?"

"More eyes on a big facility. I'm looking for something, not sure what. I don't have your gift of charm, so you might be able to get info I cannot. And ... well, maybe I'll know more when you get here."

"Gotta love a mystery. I'm blowing this taco stand as we speak. Tell me where to meet you."

Barnaby gave his old friend directions, then strolled into the hospital's human resources department in the basement. After filling out an application for janitorial services, he gave his military credentials and his commanding officer as a reference. In no time, he had a job, starting the next day at 7 a.m. if he wanted it.

Yes! His screaming instincts yearned to search the building immediately.

But he needed to wait until morning. He'd mop every floor in the place if it allowed him to figure out what his sixth sense wanted him to know.

Maybe he'd lost his mind.

Didn't matter. Work started tomorrow.

• • •

What Jane would give to wipe away the dried sweat on her forehead and the piece of hair that had crept into her mouth. It was driving her crazy.

Unfortunately, the leather restraints on the hospital bed made any movement impossible.

What she really wanted was to take a scalding hot bath and scrub her body until the skin came off. At least all of the awful cramping and bleeding had stopped, thank God.

To crush her optimism, a wave of sweat and lower belly pain steamrolled her until she cried out. Her voice had become pitiful, foreign, and thin, like an animal that had been kicked one too many times. At least she had regained her voice. She'd screamed herself hoarse however many days or weeks ago when she had first arrived here.

Where was *here*?

She squinted up at an aluminum light fixture encasing a single harsh bulb. The brightness invaded, even with her eyes closed. Every minute felt like high noon. No day, no night. Just endless light.

Tugging against the restraints, she tamped down panic. When she tilted her head back to view the room, dizziness hit her and she had to swallow hard. Maybe someone would come looking for her.

Who? She had no family. No acquaintances, due to her work. And the DEA had wiped its hands of her. For all the DEA knew, she was on the beach, sipping a piña colada and working on her tan.

Mission failure.

After the nausea passed, she cracked open her eyes once more and took in the plain, white walls encasing a plain room, devoid of any furniture save the bed on which she lay. Lime-green vinyl floors and a stinging antiseptic smell didn't reassure her. Nor did the solid-looking door with metal gridded into the inset window.

Another bout of pain gripped her lower pelvis, like the worst menstrual cramp in the universe, and she gritted her teeth until it passed.

Time meant nothing. Could have been minutes or hours.

Muffled noises in the hall tantalized her as she strained to make out the sounds. Inhuman yelps and howls raised the hair on her arms.

The door squeaked open, and she tensed. A woman entered the room carrying two syringes. Her perfectly coiffed salt-and-pepper bouffant, better suited to 1960 than today, cradled a crisp nurse's cap.

Jane pulled halfheartedly against the restraints. "Where am I?"

The nurse pushed slanted glasses up her nose. "In the hospital, of course."

"Which hospital? What happened?"

The woman made a face and ignored the first question. "Because you are committed."

"Why? I'm not crazy."

"Of course, dear." Her words didn't match the eye roll.

Jane licked her dry lips. "Why am I tied down?"

"For your safety."

"What's going on ... in my stomach?"

"Yes, well, you have a bit of an infection from, um, the infection. Well ..."

"Infection?"

The woman glanced around, and a tiny iota of sympathy flitted across her severe features. "You lost the baby."

"Baby? What?"

Oh God. In a rush, images blasted in and out of her mind, like a Super 8 movie at the end of the reel. Flip, flip, flip. Light, shadow, specks. New images piled on top of old ones until she couldn't tell where reality started and her imagination stopped.

The nurse's cold pat on the arm brought her back to reality. "My dear, you lost the baby. Your husband, Mr. Thompson, brought you here, but you were out of your mind. He thought it would be better if you received treatment in the psych unit. For your own safety."

"No. That's wrong." Jane frowned. "I'm not crazy, and I'm not married." A flash of recognition hit her, and panic choked her. "Oh my God. He's a bad man. Please, I need to get out of here."

"Oh, no. You're not going anywhere. Mr. Thompson is one of our hospital benefactors, and he's very concerned for your welfare." She lifted the syringe and flicked a bead of liquid from the tip of a long needle.

"What are you giving me?" Her heart pounded.

"Something to help with your anxiety. And something for the infection." She swabbed Jane's upper arm and arced the first syringe down to bite into muscle.

"Please. I need— What day is it?" The world fuzzed around the edges, but Jane fought to stay conscious.

"July 10, 1974, of course."

She'd lost three months?

"How long have I been in the hospital?"

"A little over a week. Treatment has been ... challenging. We were waiting for you to get over that infection so you'd be strong enough for ECT."

She struggled against the medication fog. "ECT?"

"Electroconvulsive therapy."

"You're going to shock my brain?" Breathing became difficult.

"Yes, so you don't say those crazy things anymore."

"About what?"

"Silly things about Mr. Thompson being a criminal. And how the government is involved."

Oh God, what else had she said?

The nurse sighed. "He's such a patient and loving man who hasn't given up on you. He's even coming by to check on you later today."

What the hell had happened to her?

Blasts of sensation smacked into her. A bedroom that smelled of sex and desperation, then his big, sweaty body laying on her, grabbing her, forcing her to ... Over and over, endless invasion clouded by drug after drug. Bad shit, burning her tongue. A pill going into her mouth and a hand holding her head until she swallowed it. And she'd let it happen, all to get the information to complete her mission.

Her mission. What a ridiculous mistake. God. Memories slid through the nurse's medication. The horrible pain, all of the bleeding while she was trapped in that room. Thompson wouldn't help her. How had she survived that house of horrors?

If Thompson suspected she was a narc, he would've let her die. So why was she alive? How had she ended up in the hospital?

A vague image formed of her crawling down the stairs and into the street. Somehow, she'd flagged down the police. Then she recalled an ambulance and a concerned Thompson.

By sheer luck, she had done the one thing possible to buy herself time and stay alive. She'd made a spectacle and thrust Thompson right in the limelight.

So why was she still alive?

Too much attention on Thompson. He had to bide his time.

Besides, he needed to find out what she knew first. Then he could kill her.

The meeting with Thompson today.

With an extra dose of medication and a sprinkle of plausible deniability, just like that, there would be no more Jane. She yanked at the unyielding restraints.

If Thompson didn't finish her off, then the mole in the DEA would figure out how to get rid of her. Implicating a member of the DEA as participating in a cult financed by drugs would destroy the entire organization. If the DEA went under, they'd take her with them.

Her breathing came fast and harsh as the drug took over and mixed with bare fear.

Then psychedelic swirls of light, the sharp scent of rubbing alcohol, and mindless pain in her gut created a wild howl of confusion that blended poorly with whatever the nurse had given her. Confusion blanketed her mind. The howls weren't coming from down the hall.

They were coming from Jane's own mouth.

CHAPTER 6

Barnaby swabbed the floors with a thoughtful flourish. His shoulders chafed against the starched white uniform. Did these uncivilized hospital folk never test garments on real people before distributing them to new hires?

With another slosh and a splat, he worked his way down the locked hallway. Eerie moans and screams peppered the otherwise quiet efficiency in this psychiatric ward. Such a cold environment improved no one's sanity, and even Barnaby felt mad fingers creeping up his neck at every odd sound.

Becoming a janitor had been a stroke of genius. He was like a ghost to the professionals who worked here. Even now, an older nurse with precise posture stepped out of a patient room and turned on her heel with the barest of nods to Barnaby.

Exactly as he wanted it. No impression. Blend into the bland walls and endless, same doors and rooms. Nothing interesting to see here, just a guy mopping a floor.

Only, as he passed each room, he cleaned his way over to the door and looked in each window.

He'd performed this same action hundreds of times already today, starting on the first floor as assigned. Unfortunately, his shift was drawing to an end, and he'd found nothing.

Maybe there was nothing to find.

His instincts tingled. *No. Something's here.*

Hopefully, Dante was having a productive shift as an orderly. Leave it to that oaf to land the women's health wing.

With another wet arc on the floor, Barnaby mopped his way toward another patient room.

As part of the routine, he absently peeked through glass and wire mesh.

And froze.

A gaunt figure lay on the bed, immobilized by leather straps. Bruises dotted thin legs and arms.

The patient opened her mouth as if to speak, and a low moan of despair came out.

That tone of voice was so familiar.

Shadows formed in the hollows of her cheeks, stark and severe under a harsh light.

Barnaby's heart stopped.

Jane?

Couldn't be. This person looked like a tortured POW with bony knees and a harsh angle to her jaw.

But the tangled brown hair on the pillow?

His skin turned hot then cold. His head swam. So wrong, her presence here. Even his extra sense flogged him to action. *Get her out of here!*

Z'wounds! What had been done to her?

He tried the door. Locked.

Shite. He had no idea what had happened, but he'd bet his right chestnut that she didn't belong in this wretched place.

"What are you doing, sir?"

He spun around, only to go nose to cap with the prim nurse.

Thank Christ for his gift of gab. "Good afternoon, madam. Barnie Blackstone. I'm assigned to clean this department." When he stuck out his hand, the woman edged back and frowned.

"People like you don't go in these rooms." Cold fish had more personality than this ... woman. He checked her hands. No ring. No surprise.

"Ah, my fault. Well, then, I'll carry on."

"I didn't hear about anyone new being sent here. And I know everything in this department."

Leaning on the end of his mop handle, he produced a rakish grin and tilted his head. It took all of his willpower not to check on Jane.

"You must be pretty important, milady."

The nurse blinked then blushed. She stood even straighter. "Well, yes. I've been in charge here for at least two years."

"Whoo whee. I bet you know a lot of stuff." For good measure, he bent his arms, showing off his biceps right at her eye level. It had been quite some time since he'd needed to use such overt flirtation, and he didn't know how it would work in the modern age.

She darted a tongue to lick her lips.

Four hundred–plus years old and he still had talents.

Patting the lapels of her white-buttoned dress, she smiled. "Why yes, I even know about important people coming in here."

He modulated his voice to a low purr. Dante, the typical Casanova, would be so proud of Barnaby's powers of sensual manipulation. "Even more important than you? No way."

"Oh yes, tonight we're expecting a visit from one of the hospital benefactors."

"What's a benefactor?" He rubbed his thumb over his mouth and mentally patted himself on the back when her lips parted.

"Someone who has lots of money that they've given to the hospital. We treat this man's family very well."

Barnaby didn't miss how her eyes flitted to Jane's door and back.

"Wow. Who's coming?"

"You know I can't give out that information." The woman attempted a giggle, but it came out high-pitched, too eager.

He straightened up and flexed his muscled chest. By Jove, Dante would be so much better at this game. Oh well. Beggars and choosers.

"As if I would tell anyone." He grinned. "Look at me."

She did.

Barnaby's heart thudded while she patted her stiff hair.

"Well, I suppose it wouldn't hurt to say."

"Of course not, my lovely."

Her lashes fluttered then she peeked up at him from under them. She glanced up and down the hallways. Empty.

"In this room is a VIP: the wife of Tim Thompson. You've heard of him, right?"

Barnaby nodded.

The woman pressed a bony hand to her chest. "He's amazing, you know, how he can cut through the layers of people and reveal the truth." The woman's eyes turned glassy. "No one understands the world like Mr. Thompson. If we follow his teachings, we'll all ascend to a higher plane of existence one day."

Barnaby might have been born over four centuries ago, but he'd heard enough news and local gossip to know Tim Thompson ran a huge organization called the People's Palace. A cult, maybe doing illegal drugs, but no one could pin anything down. The guy was like a slippery eel. Sure convenient that he had a devotee running the psych ward.

Then it hit him.

The zaps of his sixth sense all but grabbed his head and wrenched it back toward the emaciated figure on the bed. With effort, he kept his eyes on the nurse.

Jane? Thompson's wife?

Never let it be said that Barnaby would ever steal a man's wife.

But Jane as Thompson's wife? Lying here in the psych ward? Looking as sick as she did?

Something was dead wrong here. The air burned in his lungs.

Forming words had become difficult. His mind churned. "When is he visiting? I'll make sure this floor is sparkling." He'd rather ram the mop handle up the man's arse instead. The wood protested, and he relaxed his hands to keep from splintering the cleaning implement.

"In about an hour, actually. Oh gosh! I'd better get ready." The disappointment in her eyes was replaced by avid fanaticism. "I'm hoping he'll reward my good work." She fanned herself. "He's simply amazing."

I just bet.

As the nurse whirled and hurried to the end of the hall, Barnaby chanced another glance into Jane's room. She rolled her head from side to side.

Maybe she was the man's wife. Maybe she'd had a nervous breakdown. Who was he to judge?

Her skeletal face turned back toward the door, and one ocean-blue eye cracked open.

He caught the barest whiff of a subtle floral scent, like the yellow apricot flowers in Saigon. Or maybe it was his imagination.

But the very real voice that reached out to him through the door hobbled him like a hammer to the knees.

"Help me."

CHAPTER 7

In her dreams, Jane saw Barnaby. Of course that was impossible, but for a few seconds, the vision of his handsome face took away the pieces of her hell-filled memory.

No more pain, no more drugs, no more undercover mission, no more of Thompson's sweaty face bouncing while he ... God, she couldn't even process it all. The relentless medication meant she didn't have to figure everything out right now. Couldn't.

As the fog retook her consciousness, her last image was of familiar blue eyes and handsome brows and grimly set mouth.

For the first time in ... no idea ... she relaxed.

Time and space blended and shifted.

Bright light shone over her head. Voices drifted by.

"*Herr Gud,* Barnaby, what happened?" A voice with a strange accent came from somewhere near her feet.

"I don't know. But it will never happen again." That voice, unusually hard and tight—she'd never expected to hear it again and almost wept at the comfort it brought.

When she tried to open an eye, the light blinded her. Then a shadow displaced the light.

"You're going to be fine, Jane." Sound drifted from the backlit figure. "I swear it. I'm taking you out of here."

Air blew across her face, like the door opened and closed. Damp, cool lines formed on both temples. Tears?

"Oh, dear, what did they do to you?"

Working her jaw, she could only manage an unladylike grunt.

The gown getting pulled down over her legs was followed by a rancid expletive.

Embarrassment flooded her. If she could move her hands, she'd hide herself from view. Even though her wrists were now free of the restraints, she still couldn't move the numb limbs.

Then she floated above the hated bed, suspended by two warm, strong arms.

Now out of the light, she studied the hard line of his handsome jaw, the worried expression on his face. His blue eyes searched her as if she might disappear if he looked away. As she watched, his eyes turned black.

She shook her head. Must be the drugs making her see things.

"Bring the gurney, Dante," he growled.

Footsteps and the rumbling of wheels sounded like hope right about now.

"This shit is bad juju, dude. What are we going to do?" the accented voice called out.

"My friend, you are going to use your charm to try to get her patient file. If you can figure out which medications she requires, obtain them. And anything else you believe she needs."

The warm supports slid out from under her as she landed on another bed. A crisp sheet slid over her body and tucked under her neck. The men, one at each end of the gurney, rolled her out of the hated room. Sound warped when the bed passed through the door into the hallway. Each bump made her cramping abdomen clench again, but she didn't care as long as the journey took her to freedom.

"What about you, Barnaby?" the big blond man asked.

"I'm going back to my place. You still know the address?"

"Yeah. The hospital going to know where you live?"

"Of course not," Barnaby snapped.

"Good."

A booming voice outside the opposite end of the hall echoed over the walls.

She knew that voice. Knew it far too well.

She twisted to her side and curled into a ball, trying to cover her face with a still-numb hand.

"Oh no," she whispered.

"Dante, buy us some time." Barnaby's voice carried an edge she'd never heard before.

"Will do, man, get going. Catch you on the flip side." Footsteps pounded away from them.

A warm pressure soothed her cheek. Barnaby's palm. His hand felt like heaven and freedom. How had he found her?

Who cared?

The bed picked up speed as the doors of rooms flew by her. Flick, flick, flick. Lifeless, hard metal doors, all the same, sped past. With each door, her chest unclenched. With each door, she was getting closer to her deliverance from this hell. But not free yet.

Right as they passed through a set of metal doors, Thompson called from the far end of the hall. "Get out of my way, jerkoff!"

"My apologies," came Dante's voice.

And the doors to the psych ward clunked closed behind her.

Barnaby pushed her down another hall; then there was a ding and a whoosh.

Just as the elevator doors closed, the roar of a pissed-off Tim Thompson curdled her blood. "Find her!"

Every muscle jumped as Barnaby stroked hair off her forehead. "If you want, he'll never touch you again. I swear it."

This time she would get the words out. "Thank. You," she whispered.

"Of course. Now, my dear, please hold perfectly still. We are going to get the hell out of here."

Why was he helping her?

Didn't matter. Barnaby was here. That's all she needed to know.

When the doors opened, the scent of gasoline and echoes of traffic matched the dim glints of vehicles. Parking garage. Twilight.

Out of the hospital. Freedom. Not yet, but close.

The sounds of engines and people on the nearby street made her gulp big lungfuls of air. She didn't care that it was polluted. She just needed to breathe not-hospital air.

Alarms exploded around them. Sirens screamed and lights flashed.

Barnaby cursed. She bounced hard as the gurney flew across the concrete. He braked so hard that she would have slid off the end of the bed if he hadn't grabbed under her arm to stop the momentum.

Her vision and brain fog cleared further. Stark reality of the situation filtered in, with all the ramifications of what they were doing. Tremors racked her body.

Still wrapped in the sheet, she was lifted into his arms. With a massive kick, he sent the bed flying to the opposite side of the garage where it crashed into a vehicle at the end of the ramp.

"Shite," he mumbled as they ducked between two cars. He cradled her on his lap as he crouched in front of a rusted truck grill.

A few moments later, footsteps flew by them.

Voices turned to shouts. The searchers had found the bed.

Twilight backlit Barnaby's face into a hard, grim profile.

The muscles in his arms and thighs bunched as he balanced her weight. With a slow, grinding twist, he removed a headlight from a vehicle.

Pounding steps and Thompson's loud voice reverberated through the garage. She pressed her lips tightly together to keep from letting out a terrified cry.

If Thompson got his hands on her again—man, she couldn't even imagine. She'd never walk away from a second meeting.

She shivered. If she could stand on her own two feet, Jane would run from this place and never stop. But little in her weakened body worked right now, and that ticked her off almost as much as the awful situation.

Dependent on someone for help, all she could do was pray that Barnaby knew what he was doing.

His voice blew over her brow like hope and promises.

"I've got an idea," he whispered.

Her shiver had nothing to do with the cool evening temperature and everything to do with the vibrations of his voice rolling over her.

She'd placed her life in his hands once before, and he hadn't failed.

All those muscles bunched, like a tiger about to pounce. Instead of crouching to spring, he curled himself around her body, holding her so tightly it hurt.

Damned if she'd complain.

Footsteps came closer and stopped two cars away.

Sweat rolled down her neck.

"Someone back here?" a disembodied voice said.

With a burst of movement, Barnaby flung the headlight into the far recesses of the garage, where it shattered, drawing the searcher away.

Shouts echoed off the concrete as many sets of feet faded toward the location of the noise.

Barnaby ran, staying in front of cars, until they reached the end of the garage. Were they at ground level?

He stood up, and she peeked over the wall down a good fifty feet. Her stomach churned. Not ground level.

"Jane," a nasty voice grated.

Barnaby froze.

Thompson's boots thunked concrete as he walked out of the shadows. "Come back with me, baby. You're sick. I can take care of you, like always. We'll make more babies. Strong ones. Babies to carry on important work."

Hot stomach acid burned its way up her throat.

Barnaby frowned and glanced down at her, a silent question written on his face.

"Please, no, Barnaby. He's lying."

His curt nod gave her hope. When he studied Thompson for several seconds, Barnaby's eyebrows shot up.

"Minion? God's teeth, no," he whispered.

"What?" Jane didn't like how Barnaby had gone deathly still. Something had happened between the two men, but darned if she knew what.

Thompson grinned.

Barnaby tensed.

How would they get out of this mess?

"Let go of my wife, asshole, or I'll have you thrown in jail."

"Throw yourself in jail, Thompson," she spat. "How many crimes are enough? How much pain and suffering do you have to inflict?"

His eyes darted over his shoulder up the parking ramp. "You don't know what you're talking about, sugar. It's the drugs, of course. Look, pal, she's sick. Let me take her back for more treatment." His nice-guy act rang like a note out of tune.

A muscle jumped in Barnaby's jaw as his eyes blackened. "You will not touch her, spawn of Satan."

Thompson's expression shifted, like a curtain drawn back from his angry face to reveal pure evil beneath. By some trick of the dim light, he looked much bigger. More menacing. "You have no say in this, slave." He barked out what passed for a laugh. "You just signed her death warrant."

"Barnaby? What's he talking about?" she asked.

Barnaby glanced at the edge of the wall and then back to Jane. "He's a very bad creature. And he's lying about you being his wife."

"Yes. Every last bit of it."

He kept one eye on Thompson. "Good enough for me." Flicking a glance at Jane, he asked, "Do you trust me?"

Did she trust him? It didn't matter. Jane had just run out of choices.

"I do right now."

Several other searchers pounded concrete as they sprinted up to Thompson. The cult leader glanced at them with an uneasy expression that clouded over into one of pure hatred. His imposing frame seemed to shrink back to a normal size.

She shook her head. Must be the drugs.

Barnaby's arms tensed.

With a spring too fast to register, Barnaby vaulted the wall, and her stomach left her as they fell through air. The impact with the ground jarred her as he grunted, rolled forward onto his knees, and absorbed most of the force of the fall.

It took a minute to breathe again. "How did—?"

A roar of male anger amplified by something else nameless and evil came from three stories up.

"Shush," he said. "Let's go."

With her cradled in his arms, he ran, faster than anything she'd ever known was possible. He dodged cars, leapt benches, and ducked into an alley until they had traveled away from the garage and behind the hospital in mere seconds. They stopped near a black hearse.

How fitting.

"How—?" she asked when he stopped to study his surroundings.

As he dropped a light kiss onto her cheek, his thick brown hair brushed over her forehead. "You have your secrets. I have mine."

"But—"

"Did I fail you in Saigon?"

"No."

"I won't fail you now."

She swallowed. "Okay."

He flung open the passenger door and settled her on the seat, then ran around to the driver's side. Keys dangled from the ignition.

Because who would ever steal a hearse, right?

Apparently, Barnaby.

Jane couldn't care less.

CHAPTER 8

Barnaby had experience driving all sorts of vehicles—everything from carriages to Model Ts to tanks. But nothing compared with his attempts to make the ridiculous hearse speed to Tenderloin while still remaining inconspicuous.

He'd lost one cop car a few blocks ago, but no way would his luck hold. Likely an alert had gone out when he and Jane escaped the hospital.

Shite. A minion. Frigging bat piss. Thompson reeked of minion—a creature made by Barnaby's boss, Jerahmeel, and the worst being that could walk this earth. Minions existed to wreak havoc on the world and find new and creative ways to hurt the Indebted. Through the years, Jerahmeel somehow knew when an Indebted got too close to a human. Then boom, a minion would show up and destroy the human. Sometimes the Indebted, too, but minions typically stopped short of killing an Indebted.

Barnaby's kind could do their job without an arm or leg, but the injury would remind an Indebted to obey the boss in the future.

Ice flooded his veins. Jane was in this situation because of Barnaby. The minion wouldn't be attracted to her if she'd never come into contact with an Indebted.

By his uncle's crooked cock, when in the hell had Thompson become a minion?

To make matters worse, this particular minion wanted to make babies with Jane. Shite. Barnaby couldn't even imagine what the offspring of such evil could do. This rescue attempt had gone from chivalrous to critical in the space of a few seconds.

Z'blood, the way her tiny frame slumped in the front seat shot chills down his spine. Every few minutes, a big shudder racked her, and his own heart quaked in response. What had that minion done to her?

What hell had she suffered in that awful hospital ward?

She was ill, and Barnaby wasn't equipped to take care of someone this sick. Unexpected fear raked cold tines over his body. What if he couldn't help her? His soul wouldn't survive if he had to watch Jane die.

Would she be better off in the hospital with the treatments but also with Thompson? Or would she survive with an inadequately trained Barnaby, fueled only by fear?

His keen hearing picked up the whine of sirens. He gripped the steering wheel.

Damned if he'd let her go now.

Pushing the hearse past all factory tolerances, he clipped a curb edge and then yanked the wheel hard to avoid crashing into a parked car. The hearse floated for an unnatural second on two wheels before thudding back to full traction on the earth.

Sirens grew louder.

Barnaby had about ten blocks to get to his apartment. Could he go elsewhere? Possibly, but it would be much better to collect supplies, divest the apartment of any trace of his identity, and then clear out for good.

This vehicle would never make it to his building undetected.

His instinct for danger blazing, he whipped the hearse into an alley, careening against the two narrow brick walls until he stopped. Killing the lights, he ducked down; Jane's ragged breathing filled the vehicle.

He rested a hand on her bony shoulder, cursing when she flinched. It took every ounce of his Indebted strength to keep from bursting out of the vehicle, hunting down that wretched Thompson, and ripping the head from that minion's disgusting body. But as a warm tear hit his wrist, his attention shifted, like binocular barrels twisted until what was important came into sharp focus.

Jane.

Cop cars flew by the alley entrance, briefly shooting light and sound down the narrow passageway.

Sooner or later, someone would find the hearse. He glanced at the buildings on either side of the alley. What if someone were phoning it in to the police even now?

Time had run out.

There was not enough room to open the side doors, so he heaved his body through the back of the vehicle and stopped. No door handle. Of course not.

With a grunt, he punched through the back window and groped for the exterior handle until the door opened. Blood dripped from his knuckles and arm. He'd be fine in a few minutes.

Which was more than he could say for Jane. He clambered back to the front seat.

"My dear, we need to leave."

Her head lolled back and up until glazed eyes locked onto his like the world's strongest magnet. In the darkness of the alley, little light filtered into the vehicle, but he caught the hint of the sweaty sheen on her forehead. Was she in dire need of medical attention, or was this merely a temperature spike that would improve in a few minutes?

Damn it, he didn't know, and that scared him more than a hell-bent minion.

"Do you trust me?" He had to hear her response.

"I do right now."

Her whispered statement should have made him proud. Should have made him feel like more of a man.

Instead, it terrified him. Made him take rapid stock in his Indebted existence.

He came up woefully short.

Someone depended on him. When last had that occurred?

Fear wrapped its bony fingers around his spine.

And squeezed.

Damn it, it didn't matter how he felt. All that counted was getting Jane to safety.

"I'm going to lift you over the seats."

Her bit-off gasp when he slid his hands under her back and thin legs ruined him. Darkness shaded his vision, and at the sounds of more sirens, the instinct to protect her drove him as surely as a mad coachman with a whip.

He tried to make Jane's trip out the back of the hearse smooth, but he winced in sympathy at every jostle. In the trunk area of the vehicle, he tied the hospital sheet firmly around her waist. When she looped a thin arm around his neck, it trapped his ancient heart in his throat.

Cradling her to his chest, he exited the vehicle and scanned the area. The hairs on the back of his neck stood straight up. Flashing lights threw shadows.

Blue and red licked at each end of the alley. Several blocks from his apartment, and they were trapped.

Shite.

It would take a winged creature like the angel Gabriel swooping down to save them now.

Unless ... he could learn to fly.

He kissed Jane's clammy forehead, apologized, and draped her over his shoulder.

He vaulted to the roof of the hearse and springboarded to the lowest rung of a fire escape.

Hanging there, he adjusted her slight weight. The image of her falling onto the concrete below propelled him to heave himself up and grab one rung, then a second one. Each lurch shoved his stomach into his throat. One wrong move, and Jane would fall.

Even his immortal strength had limits, and one-armed pull-ups with deadweight attached was right at that limit.

Before he could lift a foot to the lowest rung, a police vehicle stopped at the end of the alley. The floodlight raked the darkness, casting deep, moving shadows. The jut of a building shadowed his position when the bright light swept past.

For what seemed like an eternity, they hung, suspended by his one arm above the alley.

A few minutes later, the lights blinked off, and the engine purred away.

He didn't have the luxury of a sigh of relief.

Swinging a foot up to the lowest rung, he missed, scraping against the rusted metal and then thin air.

With another ripe curse, he tried again, straining to make contact with the rung. Grunting, he leveraged himself out and up until he stood up on the bottom rung of the ladder.

Then he flew up the fire escape into the night.

Leaping from roof to roof, he worked his way back to the block where he lived.

"Lived." Bollocks. A sick jest for what he'd been doing these past years. Nay, these past centuries.

He tugged Jane from his shoulder to settle in his arms. He chafed her cold arms and legs until her eyes opened. Thank God, she was still conscious.

Lights blinked over the streets up the hill, west of the Tenderloin district. Police still swarmed the block where he'd parked the vehicle. They'd probably found the hearse by now.

Time, damn it. How had he gone from far too much time to not enough?

Since he met Jane.

He leaned over the edge of the roof, trying to judge an escape to the street level. Forty stories up. Too far for him to safely jump with Jane.

Jane's strangled cry made him scramble backward.

She clutched at his neck. "Don't do that!"

Right. Because she was mortal. In case he'd forgotten. "My apologies," he mumbled. Her tremors sent his guilt into overdrive.

With all her hallucinations, she probably thought he'd drop her over the edge. He checked his watch.

Nine p.m.

Stay here and wait for the later hours of night, with fewer people out on the street?

Or go now and try to get her into his apartment unnoticed?

He glanced to the street he'd have to cross.

Too many lights, too many people. Too many prying eyes from hundreds of windows.

He wedged himself into the corner of the roof and drew Jane into his embrace, tucking the sheet as tightly around her as possible. They'd stay here until the chances of detection dropped.

He hoped.

CHAPTER 9

How they'd managed to get into the building, Jane had no idea.

Several sickening drops from that last building should have killed Barnaby and her, but somewhere from the wild ride through the city streets to hanging out on a rooftop, she ended up here.

Where was "here"?

The off-white walls and beige furniture blended into a sameness that encouraged the eye to overlook all of it. No pictures, no personal memorabilia. No magazines. Nothing to indicate that this apartment belonged to anyone in particular.

At a rustling sound, she searched for the source. On the counter lay a file, and Barnaby was thumbing through it with a deepening frown. Although she hadn't moved, he cocked his head and glanced up at her. He'd changed from his white hospital uniform into a knit shirt and jeans.

"Hi." Barnaby's rich voice took away her anxiety like a match going out. After closing the folder, he flipped on the nearby radio. The funky beat of "Jungle Boogie" seemed way too peppy, but the noise provided a welcome distraction.

"How long have we been here?"

"Half hour or so. I wanted to leave, but you needed to rest and warm up first."

She shrugged. "We can go if you think it's best."

"We're okay for now. Police are searching for us, but they're not looking in this area yet."

She grimaced. Thompson and his psychotic behavior.

Barnaby approached her. "Why did Thompson want you so much, Jane?"

Could she tell him about the assignment?

Why not? Her cover was blown.

In fact, her career in intelligence had gone kaput the minute she'd dropped acid to weasel into the People's Palace. And freelancing to complete the mission? DEA would've loved that slick move. They had no idea what she'd told Thompson.

Jane didn't know what she'd said either, and that scared the hell out of her. Not to mention this assignment had nearly killed her.

So much for her having a purpose in this world.

What could she tell Barnaby?

For his heroics this evening, she'd tell him anything he wanted to know. Like it even mattered anymore.

She took a sip from the water glass Barnaby had proffered before he perched on the edge of the plain coffee table.

She handed him back the glass. "So. A lot has changed since Vietnam."

"I'll say."

"You remember that last night?"

The light in his blue eyes took her breath away, but she truly shivered when those eyes turned an odd black color. She could barely hear his low response.

"Impossible to forget."

Maybe the warmth up her neck had to do with another wave of fever? "The helicopter took me to one of the ships in the South China Sea. From there, all evacuees were transported to Guam, then flown back to the U.S."

Sinews flexed as he rested his elbows on his knees and leaned forward. "I wondered where you'd gone." His eyes faded to normal blue.

"Once back in the United States, I was given two choices: finish out my tour in the typing pool or join a new organization, the Bureau of Narcotics and Dangerous Drugs, which recently became the DEA, to fight the growing drug problem here in the country. You see, I wanted a career. I wanted something to call my own. I wanted to make a difference. The army wasn't going to do that for me."

"And this did?" His wry grin took the sting away from the truth.

She studied the brown-on-brown flannel blanket. "At first, I thought so. Unfortunately, the DEA didn't know exactly how to train women for the missions. Even women coming out of the army."

"Did your background in the military help?"

"Not much. No one knew how to set rules for operation in these types of unconventional situations. But because this People's Palace stuff was on the top of the DEA's radar and they were desperate for a high-profile bust, my training got fast-tracked, which is to say, cut short. Once I infiltrated the organization, I tried my best to complete the mission, but things didn't go as planned. The DEA fired me." Shame warmed her face. "So I went back to complete the mission on my own. Best laid plans, right?"

"What about your family? Aren't they worried about you?"

Stupid tears pricked, and she blinked hard. "They're all gone. No siblings. Parents died shortly before I went into the army. No one would have cared if I disappeared."

"I cared."

No way would she touch that comment. "Which brings up some questions. I saw you die on that rooftop in Saigon. What happened?"

Odd that he didn't meet her gaze.

"I had just stepped into the stairwell when the explosion hit."

"No. That's not right. I saw you standing right there on the roof."

His voice went hard and sharp, like the edge of a knife. "It was a crazy night. You must have been mistaken in what you saw."

But at his narrowed glare, she snapped her mouth shut on a follow-up question. Message received. "What about tonight? How did you end up at that hospital, Barnaby? Damned convenient if you ask me."

His wry smile twisted something both hopeful and uncomfortable deep in her belly.

"I'm a lucky guy. I've been spending some time in San Francisco for the past few years."

"You just happened to be working at the hospital where I was treated?"

"Stranger things have occurred."

"Let me get this straight: You didn't blow up on the roof where an explosion went off. And you're just hanging out in San Francisco for the hell of it?"

He glanced at the beige shag carpet. "I, ah, had a lot of time on my hands. Why not spend it in San Francisco?"

A heavy weight of sadness pressed on her ribcage. "Time. Got it."

"You never know who you're going to run into. It's a small world." His clipped words didn't ring true. Speech patterns changed. He was hiding something.

She motioned to her bony, worn-out body. "Are you glad you ran into your old army buddy?"

"Not in this way."

It hurt to swallow. "Yeah. I figured."

Sounds of the city filled the space while she tried to find something else to say.

Barnaby spread out his fingers as if reaching for her, then folded them into a loose fist. "What in God's name happened to you?"

Flashes of Thompson's bedroom, the scent of sweaty male, and the texture of polyester double knit made her want to claw her way out of this living room. Thank God Barnaby didn't wear Brut cologne, or she'd throw up. As it was, the more she tried to remember, the more light-headed she became.

She had no right to feel sorry for herself. She'd gone willingly into the abyss, all in the name of the mission.

Barnaby didn't need to know all the details. He'd done so much already. Adding the burden of her mangled conscience wouldn't help anything.

Besides, once she recovered, she'd get out of his life. No need to burden him any further.

"Can't talk about it. Sorry."

"Why?"

"How about, I don't *want* to talk about it?"

"I have some idea of what might have occurred, you know."

"How?"

He gestured toward the folder resting on the countertop. "My friend stole your medical file and a bunch of antibiotics."

"Wow. I only remember a few bad pieces of the last few months. What does the file say?"

"You're really sick."

"Mentally or physically?"

"Both."

"Well, then. Shouldn't you return me to the asylum?"

"Do you really want to go back there?" The quiet strength of his voice bolstered her.

"Hell. No."

"You and I both know that's not where you belong."

She shrugged. "So says the psychiatrist." Her laugh sounded pathetic. Even more so when Elton John started belting out "Don't Let the Sun Go Down on Me." Damn it, she refused to listen to the lyrics, especially during this conversation.

"What happened?"

It took all of her willpower to meet his concerned eyes. "Thompson."

"What about him?"

"He got me committed."

"Why?"

"I knew too much. About his business."

"Drugs? Other stuff?"

She gave him a sharp nod, nothing more.

"This is worse than I thought?"

"Yeah, aren't you glad you stepped into the nightmare with me?"

"Nowhere else I'd rather be."

"You're kidding."

Nope—if the serious, intense stare and tight press of his lips meant anything, Barnaby was dead serious.

She played with the sateen edge of the blanket. "Anyway. I'm fine now."

"No, you're not."

Her head whipped up. "What are you talking about?"

"Thompson's not going to stop until he finds you."

She sucked in a big, tepid breath, and it tasted like failure. "I know he won't stop. Man, tonight, it was like Thompson had become possessed. I've never seen him that mean."

He didn't meet her eyes. "He's more dangerous than you can imagine."

"How would you know?"

"I just know things, okay? Our best bet is for you to disappear from anyone's radar."

There was that painful truth again, but Barnaby was right. Her best hope was getting the hell out of here. Unfortunately, she could barely raise her arms, much less stand and run.

If she waited here, eventually Thompson would find her. Then what? She shuddered.

"You shouldn't be mixed up in my mess, Barnaby."

His eyes hardened like cold, blue diamonds. "You want to deal with this on your own?"

"No, but—"

"Then you'll let me help until you get stronger."

"Yes, but—"

"Do you want me to force-feed you oxtail soup?"

"What? Gross. No way."

"Then you work on getting better. Best you let me help."

"But why?"

He ran a hand through his light brown hair. Opened his mouth then closed it. "I just do."

"That's a lie."

His sigh told more of a tale than his words. "Look, why don't we focus on you? It seems like you might want to clean up."

Meaning she was unclean. She couldn't disagree.

He added, "You're also due for another dose of medication."

Her head whipped around. "Not the psych med?" Pain and horror threatened to drown her.

His warm hand on her arm anchored her to reality. "Only the antibiotic. Promise."

"Okay, then. Sure." When she rotated to a sitting position, her head swam. Where was the stupid bathroom? It would take an act of Congress to make it there.

Before she tried to stand, Barnaby's arms were under her, lifting her. His quick strides took her to the bathroom. He kicked the toilet seat down and sat her on it.

In no time, he had the tub filled with temptingly steamy water. What she'd give to scrub the hell out of her skin. Scour the flesh until she eliminated the taint of what Thompson had done to her. Unfortunately, her wounds went deeper than the skin. Maybe a sandblaster would work better.

"So, um…" Barnaby's calm voice broke her reverie.

"Yes?"

"You'll need to … get out of your clothes to get in … because …" His thick neck reddened.

It probably matched her cheeks. "I'll be okay. You can leave." That came out all wrong, as the pull at the corners of his mouth attested.

"I won't—I can help you."

"No thank you, Barnaby." Even though she said it as kindly as possible, there was no way to wipe the disappointed furrow from his brow.

"Right." He flicked a thumb toward the door. "I'll be just outside, so ..." The poor man backed away and eased the door closed.

In the stillness of the warm bathroom, Jane finally released the blanket. Her ragged and dirty nails gave some indication of her personal hell these past few months. With the last bit of strength, she untied the gown and dropped her underwear on the bathroom floor. Thank goodness, no more blood.

There was more wrong with her, though. More than an infection. More ...

Oh God, another red flash of light and pain.

Her belly clenched with real-time pain and echoes of what had come before.

Laying for days in that bedroom. Feverish pain and far too much blood.

Without the benefit of antipsychotic meds, reality blasted her with both barrels. She'd been pregnant.

And now she wasn't. Jane rubbed the skin of her hollow belly that sagged like a web between her jutting hipbones.

She covered the sob breaking out of her throat.

Remembered stabs of pain drove her to her knees next to the tub. The memory of days upon days of endless agony, begging for help, and bleeding until it was impossible for one person—much less two—to survive.

A knock at the door startled her back to reality.

"Are you all right?" Damn Barnaby's kind voice. He had no idea.

Actually, he did. He had read her medical file.

Damn it.

"Fine, just fine." The tone was wrong—too high and flat—but it would have to do.

Silence. He must have walked away. Smart man.

With a graceless heave, she flopped over the edge of the tub. Hot water flashed over her, taking her breath away. Then the warmth seeped into her muscles until she relaxed.

Unwilling to simply lay there, she soaped up and scrubbed, over and over. Her arms burned with the effort to lift the washcloth, but no way would she stop now. Over her legs, her flat belly. Over the points of bone protruding from under her thin skin. She scrubbed until lines of red bloomed over her skin. Still, it wasn't enough.

When she dipped the cloth lower, the only thing good about that pass was that no taint could be seen. Still, she felt filthy.

Clean. She had to get clean. Didn't care that there was nothing on the washcloth, she had to make sure nothing of Thompson remained.

With about a hundred baths, maybe she could make her skin clean again.

But what about her soul? No amount of soap and scrubbing would fix that wrecked mess.

She tried to wash her hair but gave up when her burning arms failed her. With an overwhelming rush, the tears flowed and she couldn't stop her sobs. Pressing her fists to her mouth, she fought to stay silent. On an audible gulp, she froze.

"Jane?"

No. Please.

"Jane, do you need help?"

She couldn't answer without sobbing.

The door creaked open.

Oh, no.

CHAPTER 10

The image burned into his mind like acid etching a pane of glass.

Jane sat, hunched over, head bowed, in the tub. Her thin shoulders shook with each deep gasp, but she made no sound. With her arms locked around her bent knees, she had curled into herself.

Not that he blamed her after what had happened. Although the medical records contained sparse information, he could read between the lines. Before him sat a strong woman who had been completely devastated, physically and emotionally.

Barnaby would die a thousand deaths before anyone hurt Jane again.

The wave of rage and protectiveness stunned him stupid.

Powerless to help, Barnaby could only look at her bent head. The depth of her sadness and his own inability to fix this problem froze him in place.

Well, as they said, out of the frying pan, into the fire.

"I'm going to help you, Jane. I won't hurt you, I swear. Okay?"

A sniff and a shaky wave of her hand would have to count for a green light.

He knelt down to move her clothes and the blanket.

"Don't touch those!" she yelled.

Jumping back, he pressed against the towel rack. "All right. Can I push them out of the way?"

She nodded.

With deliberate movements, he used the toe of his shoe to kick the material into the corner, behind the toilet. He'd burn everything, his own clothes included, everything from this apartment, if she wished.

"Tell me what I can do, Jane," he whispered.

He had to strain to hear, as she still had her face buried between her fragile arms and pressed onto her bent knees.

"I can't get my hair clean."

"Hair?"

"Yes." The misery infused into the word grabbed his heart and squeezed.

"Hair." He frantically scanned the bathroom. "Hair." He'd turned into a parroting imbecile. "No problem. We'll get you cleaned up, right as rain."

He dashed out to the living room and fished through the bag of toiletries Dante had dropped off. By Jove, Dante had thought of everything. A pink bottle. Contents smelled like flowers. Women's shampoo. Bless that big Swede.

Running back into the bathroom like he carried a grenade about to blow, Barnaby crouched near the head of the tub. Keeping himself pressed tightly to the wall, he tried to shove his body into a nonthreatening shape.

Jane's shoulder blades pressed out from under her pale skin, and he could count every single bone in her spine. The soft curves he'd recalled from Saigon were long gone, replaced by a tortured, thin frame. On her left hip below the waterline was a red mark. A red *T*.

Shite.

A brand? That whoreson frigging branded her?

His vision turned as red as her puckered skin, and it took every ounce of willpower not to turn around and hunt down Thompson and brand every inch of skin on that sick minion. Did Thompson do it before or after he turned minion?

Didn't matter.

If Barnaby ever had the chance, he'd annihilate that creature. Minion. Criminy. Minion.

Which meant Jerahmeel had become too interested in the human happenings in San Francisco. Minions had one job: Keep the Indebted focused by any means on obtaining kills to feed Jerahmeel via that damned knife.

Which meant Jane's life hung in the balance unless Barnaby could get her to safety and destroy Thompson, if such a thing were even possible. Or Barnaby could break the Indebted contract and remove himself from the payroll, so to speak. Damn that mess in Vietnam, but he needed to get over there and look at those scrolls.

In the act of storming out of the bathroom to go hunt down a minion, Barnaby turned and stopped cold, pinned in place by the ocean-blue of Jane's haunted eyes.

The shimmering fear and despair sucker punched him back to reality.

He grabbed a cup off the sink and dropped to his knees.

Praying that his touch could bring succor, even with the rage swirling inside his mind, he stroked her hair until she relaxed back into his hand. He lifted the cup full of bathwater up and rinsed. Over and over, he lost himself in the smoothness of her hair as the water sluiced through the dark brown strands.

Opening the bottle, he squeezed a dollop of scented shampoo, worked it into her scalp, and ran it through the length of her hair. Another several passes with the cup of water, and her hair was shiny and clean. For a long minute, he sat between the tub and the wall, not sure what to do next but too scared to move.

She gave a sad, weary sigh.

"Can I help—?"

"Thank you, Barnaby—" she blurted at the same time.

He clamped his jaw shut and tried again. "Let's get you out of here before you turn into a prune."

The lift to the corner of her sweet mouth would have to count as a smile. Grabbing another towel, he held it out.

"I d-don't want y-you to—" she stammered.

When her lower lip quivered, he was lost.

"Verily, I won't look."

When she glanced at the towel, she raised an eyebrow. "I don't have anything to wear, and that's not going to work."

"Right."

He dashed out of the bathroom, ripped off a sheet from his rarely used bed, and skidded to a stop back in the bathroom.

"Better?" he asked.

Her harsh laugh did him a world of good.

"I'll help you to the edge of the tub and dry you off. No looking, I promise."

"Fine." The flatness of her voice hurt.

She weighed almost nothing as he lifted her to the ceramic rim and toweled her back and arms dry. Draping the sheet over her shoulders, he removed the towel from beneath and eased her into a sitting position on the bathroom floor. There, he toweled her hair dry. She clutched the sheet around her.

"Better?" he asked.

When she angled her face up and back and gave him a glimmer of a smile, his heart swelled in his chest.

"Yes, better. Thank you."

"Um, how about back to the couch?"

"Okay."

He didn't miss how her damp head tucked into the space between his shoulder and neck made him feel complete, purposeful.

Too bad he had no purpose except to carry out his Indebted contract.

Too bad the only thing that made him complete was slaking that damned knife's hunger.

He was a monster crammed into the shell of a man. Nothing more.

• • •

Jane shrunk back away from the syringe Barnaby brandished.

He stepped back and raised his hands. "Antibiotics. I swear. You need it for, the, um, infection."

"It's okay. I know what happened. The miscarriage had complications."

He looked everywhere but at her. Jane didn't blame him.

"So, may I?" He waved the wicked-looking needle.

"Doesn't matter," she said, slipping her arm out from under the sheet. As the bite of metal and tight squirt of liquid hit her upper arm, she felt a burn low in her pelvis. That's what failure felt like, no doubt.

After wiping the tiny drop of blood on her upper arm, he set the syringe on the coffee table. "So. Sure it's Thompson's?"

"The miscarriage? Yeah." She sure was doing a great job memorizing the bland pattern on the couch cushions tonight. "Change the subject, please."

"Right. Bad choice of topic." He paused long enough for her to glance over and check on him. Myriad emotions—everything from sadness to curiosity to banked, lethal anger—shone from his eyes. "So are you ready to get out of here? Even though the police haven't made it to this block yet, doesn't mean they won't soon. Any idea where you want to go?"

"I have no place to go. The DEA won't take me back; I'm compromised, a liability, after everything."

"That's not true."

"Well, then, let's just say I don't want to deal with the DEA right now."

"Fair enough."

"Actually, I'd like to somehow get that info to the DEA chief, who might believe me, about the drugs and sex trade. If those women are suffering as much as than I did, they have to be freed. Also, I think my supervisor was somehow involved."

"Okay then." The line of his jaw turned to hard rock. "Why don't we put together a plan to inform him after you're healed?"

"Sure."

"So. No idea ...?"

"I don't have a home. No family. So that leaves a whole lot of nothing." She swallowed around the lump in her throat.

"Or a lot of possibilities." A smile lit up his handsome face.

For the first time in months, her heart lifted. A foreign feeling. Hope. "Yeah?"

"Yes. I have an idea."

"Your last idea landed me forty stories up on a roof." She smiled as he pulled a face. "But let's hear it."

"I have a little place in the Santa Cruz mountains. No one knows about it. You'll be safe."

"Barnaby, I can't impose."

"If you were imposing, I wouldn't offer." His voice, so grave, made her want to burst into tears all over again.

"I don't know ..."

"Do you trust me?"

The $64,000 question again. No doubt about her answer at this point.

Her pathetic attempt at a laugh made her even sadder. "What choice do I have?"

The next half hour faded into a blur of Barnaby's energetic activity, phone calls with mumbled conversations, and her own exhaustion.

At one point, his constant motion stopped when he stood over her, his arms filled to bursting with bags and supplies.

"I'm going to pack up the car. I'll be back in a few minutes."

She'd be here alone? Her heart thudded. Who was she to complain? It wasn't as though she had many choices. "No problem."

When he dashed out of the room, the emptiness around her felt like a mantle of fear and failure. She huddled, spine rigid, with the sheets clutched about her curled frame.

Until the door exploded inward.

She yelped, and a wave of sweat fired through her.

Chuck leered at her from the hallway.

Murmurs of nearby tenants drifted down to her, but the big man storming over to her consumed most of her senses.

"What are you ... how ...?" she managed.

"That stupid janitor used a fake address on his job application at the hospital, but one of his references had this address listed. What an idiot. Once we realized who kidnapped you, Thompson sent me here to ... get you out of here."

He pulled a compact pistol. A Sig Sauer, if her weapons training remained relevant.

Relevant for the next few seconds, at least.

Jane's stomach dropped out from under her.

Chuck snorted. "We tried the nice way to get you to shut up."

"What? By drugging me into oblivion?" She didn't care if she riled him. Thompson and his cronies had taken everything. The least they could do was provide some answers before killing her.

"Thompson wanted to know what you told the DEA so he could plan his next business move, but at this point, screw that. Damn idiot still wanted you alive to try to make more little Thompsons. Go figure. In my opinion, he should have killed you at the very beginning. Doesn't matter now. You're history. Problem solved." He chuckled. "Killed escaping the loony bin."

The big man took one step closer. Then another. The rock rhythm of BTO's "Takin' Care of Business" punctuated his steps. Fitting.

She flexed, testing her muscle strength. Not much defense to offer other than flopping to the floor.

With any luck, Chuck would throw his back out bending over to shoot her.

No such luck.

What an inglorious end to her career. Shot dead, wrapped in nothing but a sheet. When they did the autopsy, they'd find her hopped up on antibiotics with traces of God-knew-what drugs in her bloodstream. They'd know she was recovering from a horrendous miscarriage, so maybe chalk it up to hormones making her crazy. The DEA would label her a rogue, and rightly so, and then ... what?

Nothing.

Nowhere to send her body.

No one to mourn.

How had her life come down to this pathetic end?

What about Barnaby? He was about to walk into the barrel of Chuck's gun.

The nasty man flicked the safety and aimed.

"Say bye-bye, honey."

"No, wait!" she shouted.

He froze for only a moment, but that's all that was needed.

In a blur she couldn't follow, Barnaby flew through the open door and hit the man like a vertical projectile. The gun fired, and the couch shuddered as a puff of fiberfill and fabric drifted out of a hole in the cushion.

Her right ear rang, but she could still hear snapping bones and screams.

Another gunshot and Barnaby rolled away, blood coating the front of his shirt. He didn't move.

Oh God, Barnaby.

Chuck staggered back to his feet, fumbling for the gun with the hand that wasn't attached to a broken arm.

"I've killed him. Now you're next," he growled.

His arm shook as he raised the gun once more.

Well, that was it.

Life, nice while it lasted.

Actually, no, it kind of sucked eggs while it lasted. Maybe death would be better.

Before she had a chance to test her theory, Barnaby sprang like a tightly coiled Lazarus, smacking the gun to the floor and grabbing the man's broken arm until Chuck collapsed with a howl.

Barnaby reached under the hem of his Levi's and extracted a dangerous-looking knife.

The blade glowed green.

As he flicked a glance up at Jane and then back to Chuck, she caught the eerie green glow of the knife reflected in Barnaby's black eyes. She froze.

Growling, he sat on top of the man. He grabbed Chuck's jaw and turned it so the man had no choice but to look with horror at Barnaby's rictus of a grin.

"You will never hurt her," Barnaby snarled.

Chuck mumbled something she couldn't hear.

"Don't care," Barnaby said.

And plunged the knife hilt-deep into the man's chest, then twisted.

He shoved his hand over Chuck's scream and rode the twitching body for a few seconds until the man didn't move.

It wasn't until Barnaby swiveled his head around to stare at Jane that she realized she'd clapped her own hands over her open mouth.

The brief flicker of ecstasy on Barnaby's face as he closed his eyes and sighed made her nauseous.

With an efficiency of movement that suggested this wasn't the first time he'd made this move, Barnaby used the dead man's pants to clean the blade and slid the knife back into the sheath on his leg.

"Let's go."

"What?"

He couldn't be serious. Go with him? Who was he? What was he? Nothing about Barnaby felt completely human. Not the speed of his attack, not his bizarre strength. And certainly not the part where he had been resurrected from a point-blank gunshot to the chest.

She should be calling for help.

And then what?

Shouts and doors slamming brought her back to reality.

She had limited choices, and none were good.

"Jane." Still kneeling on the floor over the silent body, he held a bloody hand out to her. "Please, I want to help you."

She shook her head. "By doing ... this?"

"If I have to, yes. I was prepared to do the same thing in Vietnam if it meant keeping you safe."

Oh God. "What? ... how? ... what are you?" Her mind couldn't even form the questions that needed to be asked.

"I can't— Shite. Please believe that I would never hurt you." He stared at his hand and wiped it on his pants, as though that would somehow help.

"I don't know."

Footsteps pounded down the hall.

"Jane, please."

This moment, right here, with Jane wrapped in a sheet on a beige couch in a beige room of a supernaturally strong man who killed people—this moment was where the two paths of her life waited. She'd picked a bad path before. So what about now? She could take the leap of faith with a killer who had kept her safe in ungodly situations or stay here, go to the police, and risk Thompson, commitment, and death.

Not so big of a choice, when put that way.

CHAPTER 11

Hours later, the rays of dawn lit up the twisting roads near Santa Cruz. Barnaby pulled the bronze Nova into the local sundry store. He had changed the bloody shirt before leaving the apartment. No need to attract unwanted attention. With a light touch on Jane's arm to alert her, he tucked his jacket more firmly around her shoulders and locked her in the car.

Leaving her alone was the last thing he wanted to do, but he had to get supplies and try to make her comfortable in this hellish situation.

A situation he'd precipitated.

If only he hadn't connected with her in Vietnam, if only he'd followed through on his promise to find her in San Francisco, Jane wouldn't be a broken and ill woman. He had one job—to search for her—and he couldn't be bothered to do it.

Look what happened. She'd almost died. A minion still tracked her.

What a worthless bastard. And he didn't mean the minion.

Inside, he picked up several weeks' worth of dry goods and a few outfits he thought might suit Jane. Later this week, Dante would drop off a bag of women's clothes and additional supplies at the store.

Even his old friend didn't know the exact location of the mountain retreat, and Barnaby liked it that way.

With a bare nod at the young worker who raised her eyebrow at the order, Barnaby paid and hurried back out to the car.

His whole life, such as one could call it, was in this vehicle.

Did that include Jane?

What a wretch, but he couldn't follow that thought to its terrible conclusion. He had to live in the here and now, as he had for the past 400 years.

If only he could stop this hamster wheel from hell. The urge, the kills with that cursed knife, the relief, the hope that he might have completed the contract, and then despair. Always ending on despair. Rinse and repeat.

If he'd returned to Vietnam, he might have found those scrolls. Might have broken the curse by now.

But then again, he wouldn't have found Jane and saved her from Thompson.

Then again, if he hadn't encountered Jane in the first place, the minion wouldn't have been drawn to her and wouldn't have hurt her.

Ah, shite. No answer worked.

Steering the car up the highway, he turned onto an unmarked dirt road. He prayed that the road was clear of debris, as it had been more than a year since he'd come up here.

After traveling several miles deep into the forest, he parked in front of his cabin. In the late morning light, the redwood-sided cabin thrust a porch off the steep mountainside and suspended it into the pale blue sky above the pine trees. The familiar lines of Loma Yorba's rocky peak to the north soothed him. He so loved nature, loved having a place apart from his sick existence as an Indebted.

Sadly, though, the peace never lasted. Not as long as he had to kill criminals on demand.

Couldn't rightly do that up here, alone in the woods, now, could he?

Before getting out of the car, he woke Jane with a gentle rock to her shoulder. Even then, she startled, her aqua eyes going round until she focused on him, blinked, and relaxed. He may never know more than a fraction of what she'd been through, but he knew what reliving past traumas looked like, and right now, fear was written all over her lovely face.

"We're here," he said.

Yawning, she glanced around. "Wow. Beautiful." She pulled the door handle.

He rushed over to help her out of the car. Sure enough, her attempt to stand failed, and he swept her up again.

"Sorry," she mumbled, giving a vague motion that encompassed the sheet still wrapped around her, the car door, and her legs.

"You've nothing to be sorry about. Ever." He shifted her into what he hoped was a more comfortable position. Sure as hell was making him uncomfortable, her proximity. Which made him even more of an evil bastard. Maybe he had a reputation as a paramour over the centuries, but no way would Barnaby hit on a convalescing woman.

He breathed in the air, still warm at the end of July, but lighter here in the mountains. Douglas firs and redwoods dominated the chaparral scrub oaks with their rich green leaves shifting in the breeze.

"I hope you like it here."

Her smile, a rare treasure, lit up her face, giving him a glimpse of what heaven must look like. "I already do. Thank you for everything."

All of a sudden, something irritated his eyes. "Yes, well. Take a moment to change into this outfit, and I'll give you the grand tour. Then it's time for your next dose of antibiotic and for you to rest."

When her face fell, he cursed at himself for being such a fool. Great job, reminding her of the trauma. But he'd caused this mess, so he would finish his job and see her healed. He owed her at least that much.

Then he'd leave her the hell alone.

• • •

Jane loved the cabin. Loved how she could view miles of mountains from the airy porch. The redwood plank walls and floor gave it a welcoming, burnt-orange glow. She could breathe in the wood scent of the house, Barnaby's masculine scent, and the fresh air every day of her life and be a happy woman.

Too bad her future didn't include a cabin and happiness.

And it sure as heck didn't include a normal, kind man ... or even a freakishly strong killer.

God, what a mess.

She sat in her position of choice, curled up on a couch with Barnaby nearby. Better to keep an eye on him. He still had that knife strapped to him.

The fleecy softness of the velour tracksuit he'd bought at the store didn't fit right. It hung off her bony frame, reminding her of all that she'd lost.

After quelling a wave of self-pity and then paranoia, she sipped at the double-strength hot chocolate he'd insisted she drink.

She studied his handsome face, knitted tight in concentration, as he puttered around the cabin, putting away food supplies and items he'd removed from his apartment. How did he go from cold-blooded killer to domestic engineer?

And how could he function after being shot point-blank in the apartment? Nothing made sense, and the ends of her frazzled nerves kept buzzing. It didn't take a background in pattern recognition to know that something didn't add up.

The least she could do for both herself and Barnaby was to recuperate quickly and get out of his life and re-create her own.

"Penny for your thoughts?"

She jumped out of her skin. How long had he been watching her?

"Just taking everything in," she hedged.

At his intake of breath, she figured he would say something, but he clamped his lips together for a full minute. "All right then. So. I have plans to feed you until you burst tonight. Until then, let's get you up and moving."

In spite of herself, Jane smiled. "What did you have in mind?"

"Nine-mile hike in the mountains." When he winked, her heart flopped. "Just kidding. How about taking a few steps around the living room?"

Sitting up, she gave him a thumbs-up. "I'll do anything to get better."

Was that a shadow of a frown below the sweep of thick, brown hair?

"Well, let's get some music to help you along." He tuned the countertop radio to a Top 40 station.

Ah yes, "The Loco-Motion" by Grand Funk Railroad. Perfect.

He turned to her. "Right, then. Let's see what you can do, turbojet."

Ten wobbly steps later, and Jane's energy had deserted her. Even with Barnaby at her side, she nearly hit the floor when her legs gave out on that tenth step. Like it was no big deal that an adult couldn't walk, he tucked her into his side and shuffled her back over to the couch.

Damn it, but her legs trembled like she was a newborn foal, and all she wanted to do was sleep for hours. A year of insane levels of stress and several weeks of a life-threatening condition ending in full restraints would do that to a person.

He returned to the couch with a quilt, which he tucked around her. Cocooned in the fleece, the warm, woody scent, and the thick fabric, Jane's tension seeped away for the first time in as long as she could remember.

Unfortunately, she slept.

CHAPTER 12

Typically, when he visited his mountain retreat, Barnaby relished the lack of connection with humanity.

Now? It scared the hell out of him.

Nothing, not disease, not pestilence, not war, and not even death itself, scared Barnaby. Until now.

Sure, he had his uncanny instinct for danger, but it meant nothing if an army stormed the cabin.

Fear, foreign and unsettling, churned in his gut. He paced from the kitchen to the porch, peering out over the once-peaceful mountains and saw nothing but opportunities for danger to hide.

At least he'd fed the knife, albeit unwittingly, with Thompson's crony. That meant Barnaby wouldn't have to leave Jane and travel to a large population center to find a criminal for about a week.

If he weren't an Indebted, he'd be free to consider a normal life with Jane. They could do mundane things like go out on a date. As it stood, the longer he and Jane were together, the danger increased.

However, if he weren't an Indebted, he wouldn't have had the preternatural strength to save her.

Criminy.

Even if she could heal to the point where she might trust someone with her heart and soul, why would a woman like Jane choose an eternal killer?

No woman would want his name on her dance card.

Barnaby was intrinsically corrupted by the evil he had performed over hundreds of years. He didn't care about the people he killed. It didn't faze him to take a meal after a kill, even with the scent of blood filling his nostrils. No amount of atonement could ever purge the taint on his soul.

The worst part of his existence? He no longer felt the modicum of justice or remorse when he stabbed a criminal. It just didn't matter.

Barnaby's connection with humanity had come undone.

Save one last tiny tether to this mortal world. One last trigger for his sixth sense. His damned power kept sitting up and pointing when it came to Jane. Maybe his extra ability was trying to tell him something.

Without Jane, he'd be adrift. Lost.

With Jane, her life would be forfeit.

He'd do anything to protect her. Even it if meant breaking the last ties he had to his humanity. Even if it meant leaving her alone. He rubbed his fists over his eyes.

Because …

No.

He eyed the darkening skies and breathed in the cool evening air that drifted through the open windows. Shaking his head, he returned to stand over Jane's sleeping form.

When he checked the clock, he did a quick calculation. Jane had slept for more than eight hours.

She needed her rest. Needed to recover.

Only, once she recovered her strength, then she'd leave.

A nasty jealousy for her health flashed by him, like a blast of flame, singeing his good sense as it blew past. He gritted his teeth against the unnatural emotion and tamped it down, like batting out a fire with his bare hands.

The radio faded in and out with the strains from Jim Croce's "Time in a Bottle."

The quilt rose and fell with Jane's slight breaths, and the evening shadows gave her face an eerie, skeletal appearance.

Because that's what she would be at the end of her natural life: a skeleton, in the ground like every other mortal.

And Barnaby would continue unto eternity his maudlin existence, numb to his kills, driven only by the knife's impulse until … what? Until nothing. He had no end to the evil.

Jane shifted and frowned, as if sensing his unsettled mood. Cursing himself as a selfish fool, he eased away from her, taking his black thoughts with him, and stood on the porch, gripping the rail. The only light in the cabin came from a single lantern on the mantel.

He had lived for more than 400 years. What had he done with his time to make this world better?

Nothing.

He had immense Indebted strength. How had he used his power to help humanity?

Save dabbling in a war here and there, he'd done nothing with it, other than impressing the ladies with his prowess in the bedchamber.

How about his fortune amassed over the centuries? Had he endowed a university or created a legacy?

No. He'd done naught with any of it.

The railing creaked under his grip, and he forced himself to relax his hands lest he destroy one of the few things in this world he cherished.

A whimper behind him made him whip around.

Had he misheard?

"No, not ... please, no ..."

He skidded to a stop next to the couch, half leaning over as a shield, his senses alert for whatever could hurt her.

In the twilight, sweat glistened on her forehead as she feebly thrashed on the couch.

"Jane?" he ventured.

A moan like an animal being tortured rent his soul in two.

"Sweetling? Are you all right?" Z'wounds, he hadn't used that endearment since his time with Bess. Not the time to think about that significance.

When Jane didn't answer, he touched her wrist, just the lightest touch.

The scream that burst from her dry lips terrified him like nothing he'd heard before on this Earth.

When it continued despite his murmured reassurances, his blood iced.

Jane's eyes were open, but she looked right through him. He could only encourage her to wake up and prevent her from falling onto the floor.

Midscream, she stopped.

And blinked.

"Barnaby?" Her hoarse voice abraded his heart like sandpaper.

"I'm right here."

He would give his own life to stop her desperate, heaving gasps. Cursing, he pulled her awkwardly onto his lap on the floor and crooned nonsense to her, repeating childhood rhymes from his youth.

When her shaking subsided, he kept rocking her and singing.

She leaned back and stared at him.

He stopped in the middle of "For Want of a Nail" and focused on the shadowed face before him.

"Hi, Jane."

"Hi. Listen, I'm so—"

"Stop. No apologies here. That's the rule."

She rubbed a damp cheek into his shirt, blessing him with the gesture.

As darkness fell in earnest, he kept her in a loose embrace, present but not confining. The last thing he wanted was to re-create any more nightmares in the dim light.

It was one of the witching hours, when day turned to full night. Barnaby sighed. So different, this modern world compared with the one he'd left centuries ago.

"Want to talk about it?" he asked after a time.

Rubbing at her arms, she shook her head. "No, I want—I want this off of me. All of it. No more darkness. No more pollution."

"What do you mean?"

"I want light. I want to be clean." She scratched at her arms, and he deflected her gently, not wanting to see her do injury.

He eased her back onto the couch and bowed. "At your service."

In no time, he had every lantern and candle lit. Bright light bounced off the walls of the cabin. A fire crackled in the grate, and he placed a large pot of water on to boil. He also fired up the propane stove and placed another pot of water on it as well.

As her opened mouth, he held his hand up, stilling her words. "Your wish is my command, milady, and I'm not done yet."

Returning from the small outbuilding, he carried a large iron tub back into the house and set it in the middle of the living room floor.

"Your bath is coming up."

"What? No, you didn't have to—"

"Who says it's for you? I don't smell so fabulous, if you hadn't noticed."

Despite her red-rimmed eyes, she giggled, the tinkling sound shaming his dark soul.

With quick work at the sink pump, he filled the tub halfway with cold water. Adding in the hot, he tested the temperature. Hopefully, it was about right.

"Oh my God, you just … did all of this? Because I asked?"

He shrugged. "Of course. Now, if you'll allow me to lay out some toiletries on this chair here, I'll leave you to your ablutions."

He helped her to one of two chairs he'd placed next to the bath. On the other chair, he set out towels, cloths, soaps, and the other clothing he'd purchased.

"Barnaby?"

"Yes, swe—Jane."

"Why did you really do all of this for me?"

"I'm not—"

"Remember? Language pattern specialist?" She cocked a thumb at her chest. "I can tell when people aren't being honest."

"No. I don't—" He dragged his hand through his hair. He owed her some explanation. Didn't have to be the entire truth, right? "Look, Jane. I'm a bad person." Raising his hand at her protest, he continued, "I've done some pretty awful things over the years. And I can't help but feel responsible for the situation you're in."

"That makes no sense. This mess isn't your fault."

"It might be."

Her eyes widened. "I don't understand."

"The bad things I've done ... have to do with Thompson being so evil. To you." Shite. He'd said it, hadn't he?

She shook her head. "How?"

"Please. I can't say more without you being in even more danger."

"More than a cult leader letting me hemorrhage to death? More than falling thirty feet from a garage? More than a maniac pointing a gun at me?" Her eyes glinted in the light.

He opened his mouth once, failed, and tried again. "Yes. More than that."

When she pressed her lips together, the flat expression on her face shredded his soul.

"Fine."

"Um, pardon?"

"Fine. You have your secrets. I get that." She eyed the steaming tub. "Now I'd really like that bath, if you don't mind." Her shaking hand contradicted the determined set to her jaw.

"Anything." He stumbled as he backed up. "I'll just be—"

"I don't want you to ... please just don't go far."

He stopped dead in his tracks, unable to answer. A few seconds later, he had a firmer grip on himself.

"Of course." He slid the glass on the porch closed and used more willpower than he possessed to turn his back on the woman inside the cabin.

CHAPTER 13

Pink, warm, and most important, scrubbed clean, Jane heaved herself from the tub to the chair and dried off. Barnaby had set out a second set of clothes. The sporty zip-top outfit made her look like the Bionic Woman, minus the super strength, of course. But she didn't care. With a sigh, she drew the pants up, her fingers bumping against the puckered skin on her hip.

The permanent reminder of her horrible decision making could never be erased.

"Barnaby?"

Faster than her eye could register, he was in front of her.

"How?" she stammered. No human could move that fast.

Shifting from one foot to another, he didn't meet her eyes. "Trick of the light." He crossed his arms over his muscled chest.

She wouldn't learn more about him tonight. "Well, ok, then. Um, thank you for the bath."

"If you don't mind giving me a moment, I'd like to do the same."

Heat climbed her neck. "Not in the water I used!"

"Yes, indeed. And you are perfectly fine, clean, and without blemish. I have no qualms using the same bathwater."

Another wave of ugly shame hit her. Of course, people had shared bathwater for ages. She hadn't done any activity today, hadn't actually required a bath.

But she had *needed* it. Had to erase the nightmare any way possible.

If Barnaby wanted to wash, after all he'd done to help her, how could she deny him?

"Yes, you're right." She darted a glance around the small cabin. "So, um, where do I need to go?"

"You can sit on the porch outside or in the bedroom over there. Your choice."

"Porch. If I need anything ..."

"I'll be there in a twinkle." He helped her walk the ten feet and settled her into a chair. "See? You're already stronger."

"All that sleep."

He held up a finger and went back into the cabin. Clanking sounds drifted through the window, until he reappeared.

"Eat, please." He handed her a glass of milk and a cheese sandwich.

Perfect.

"Thank you." Wonder Bread smelled like fine cuisine right about now. She took a generous bite and leaned her head back on the chair while she chewed.

"Enjoy the evening air. I'll be back soon."

The light kiss he dropped on her forehead drew out a shiver.

Like a whisper, he closed the door and disappeared inside.

Stars dotted the clear sky above the surrounding mountains, and a crescent moon had started to rise. Tree frogs chirped, and animals rustled in the underbrush.

A breeze ruffled through the fir trees, creating a low hum of background sound.

Yellow light shone from every window in the cabin. It blew her mind that he'd lit the place up on her say so.

Instead of relaxing her, the tiny noises and changes in air pressure set her nerves on edge.

The rustles became hinges squeaking and the creak of bedsprings, and memories of that Saigon closet and her time with Thompson rose up in her mind's eye. Terror clawed its way into her throat and threatened to strangle her.

No. She would not fall into the pit again.

Standing, she clung to the back of the oversized Adirondack chair and peeked in the window. See? Barnaby was right there, mere feet away. His big shoulders flexed as he rinsed his hair. If she called, he would be there in a second. She sank back into the chair.

She was safe.

For now.

Damn this fear. She had to purge herself of the horror, or she wouldn't be able to function. Wasn't that what they preached in training? Debrief after the mission.

Maybe, too, if something happened to her, Barnaby could still find a way to save those innocent women.

A faint splash and footsteps reached her ears.

The porch door slid open. He'd tucked a striped, long-sleeved shirt into the narrow waist of his Levi's. Both knit and denim stretched over ridges of muscles in a way that both reassured and unsettled her. He'd combed his thick hair back, and damp, it glinted in the cabin's light.

He offered her the quilt, and she wrapped it around her body.

"How are you doing?" he asked, dropping into the chair next to hers.

"Okay."

"These things take time."

A tight fist of fear squeezed until she had to concentrate to breathe. "I need to tell you what happened."

"You need to tell me, or you need to tell someone?"

An odd question, but the answer brought clarity. "Both." She paused.

"But it's scary?"

"Yes."

"All right." He didn't touch her, but the warmth in his voice wrapped around her like a comfortable sweater, not binding, but moving as she needed to move.

Swallowing, she began. "So you know how I joined the DEA and went through training? Well, I hadn't completely gotten over my fears from that night in Saigon."

"Really?"

"That night really rattled my cage. You try waiting for your death in a dark closet." She laughed. "Actually, you did, and you handled it way better than I did. Anyway, that experience scared the hell out of me, and I struggled with the need to control my own destiny afterward."

"Makes sense."

"When I was offered the job at the DEA, I figured it was a way to take charge of my life. Before I could blink, I was playing the part of a brainwashed inductee of the People's Palace, blindly following the divine teachings of Tim Thompson." His name left a foul taste in her mouth.

Rolling her neck to loosen the tight muscles, she continued. "I lost control of the mission. I didn't know how to get them to trust me without jumping in with both feet. But the DEA had strict rules about how far an agent could go. And Thompson was suspicious of anyone who didn't participate fully in the teachings ... or the drugs."

"So you participated?"

"I'm not proud that I did it. But I tried to get rid of the substances whenever possible. Participation was the only way I could gain trust and inside information about the drugs and the trafficking."

"Drug trafficking?"

She almost couldn't say the words. "Yes. And human."

"What?"

"Yeah, once I figured out what was happening, I had to get the information needed to shut down this organization, once and for all."

"Wow."

"One day, I reported in to my CO, Howard. He basically fired me on the spot for not completing my mission. But he also made comments that were wrong. He knew more than he should have." She tapped her head. "I can tell. I think he yanked me because I was about to reveal his involvement. Maybe others in the DEA were involved, too."

"So those bastards tried to run you out of the DEA?"

"Basically. But dirty rats didn't figure on my stubborn streak" She swallowed a sip of milk. It didn't calm her stomach. "I was so tired of failure that I decided to freelance the rest of the mission. Damn it, I was so close."

"Wait. You continued the job?" In the darkness, his voice carried a sharp edge.

"Idealistic? Sure. Vindictive? Maybe a little bit. Smart? Not in the least. When I got back to the house, Thompson and his second-in-command, Chuck, cornered me."

"Whoresons."

"Chuck's the guy you killed, by the way."

"Good riddance."

Scrubbing at her face, she took a big breath. "So when they caught me sneaking back in, it was a bad scene. Thompson chose that moment to share his lust for me and wanted me to become his number one wife, which isn't an honor, in case you wondered. To refuse would have been certain death, as suspicious as Thompson had become."

"So is that when—"

"Yes. I became his ... partner in April. Although my position as first wife landed me a seat at the meeting table, which yielded all kinds of good intel, most of my time was spent in a drugged haze, awaiting his ... pleasure. God, I can still hear the creak of rusty springs when he'd kneel on the bed, and ... yeah." She sniffed. "At least I found out about how the trafficking worked since he'd talk while he did things to me. Then, as you know, I became pregnant." Acid burned in her stomach, and her lower pelvis clenched. The desire to scrub herself all over again distracted her. "I feel so disgusting. So wrong. So screwed up."

"It's not your fault."

"Logically, you might be right. I had the information to take his entire organization down and reveal the mole in the DEA. But once I got thrown in the asylum, nothing mattered. I had volunteered for the mission and failed. The complicit drug use and sex ruined any credibility I had. Didn't help that I'd been fired and free-lanced the mission. And my failure meant that more women would have the same fate, or even worse. What I'd do to get those women out of there. In some ways, the miscarriage was a blessing."

She raised her hand at his protest. "If I hadn't escaped long enough to get help and force him to place me in the hospital, I would have died right there in the house."

"Good lord."

"The day you got me out of the hospital, Thompson was coming for me. I'm betting he and the DEA wanted to learn what information I had collected, and then he'd orchestrate a medical accident. Or he'd try to make me have more babies. Either option was not good."

"That's sick."

"That's how he thinks. The other weird thing was how his personality shifted during the time I knew him."

"How?" The quick way Barnaby asked suggested he knew the answer.

She shook her head. "He got angrier, harder. More intense. Not exactly more driven, but somehow bigger. Colder? More evil? It's hard to explain."

"That's a good job profiling him."

"Also part of the problem. I posed a massive security risk. So he paid off the staff at that hospital and threw me in the psychiatric ward. Good thing I was given antibiotics to go along with my tranquilizers. If that hadn't happened, I'd be dead, no question."

"I can't believe you survived."

"I can't believe you found me. You know what's funny though? I could swear I saw you on that day when Thompson and Chuck caught me. But that didn't make sense. Besides, you were dead, remember? I must've been hallucinating."

"Maybe not. For whatever reason, I was ... drawn ... to the Haight district." His voice, low and grim, sliced through the evening air. "I would have gotten you out of there if I'd known."

Her eyes burned. "How could you have known? I was deep undercover."

"I just ... should have known."

"It's not your fault, Barnaby."

"Nor is it yours that these horrible things have happened."

"I made my own decisions."

His low voice cut through the night air. "Listen to me. It's not your fault."

"Okay."

"No. Let me repeat. It's not your fault."

"Not my fault?" A fist tightened in her chest until she couldn't breathe.

"No."

That damned fist in her chest released like a spring unloading.

CHAPTER 14

In the bedroom, Barnaby sat in a straight-backed chair he'd brought in from the kitchen. He hadn't left Jane's side since her horrific story.

This woman had tried her hardest to do the right thing, and it backfired on her in the worst possible way. Khe Sanh became Saigon became Thompson's basement and then the psych ward. Nightmare blending into unending nightmare.

It took all of Barnaby's unnatural power to hold his rage in check. The last thing Jane needed was for him to scare her in an explosion of supernaturally fueled anger. Maybe one day she'd need his fury, but not tonight. Her spirit had been bent so close to the breaking point, but she still hung on.

Especially if Barnaby had anything to do with it.

Interestingly, it sounded like Thompson hadn't been a minion when Jane first arrived at People's Palace. So at some recent point, Jerahmeel had turned Thompson into an even bigger monster. How? Why?

God's teeth, Jane was in trouble.

Rubbing his eyes, he refused to consider what would happen if the minion got to her again. Barnaby just wanted to focus on the woman next to him.

If he had his wish, he'd curl up and wrap his arms around her until she woke. However, he didn't want his desperate embrace to push her into yet another nightmare of being trapped.

So he sat by her side, watching her breathe, hanging on her every sigh and murmur, and stroking her silky hair if another night terror tried to take hold.

In the darkness of the cabin, surrounded by miles of nothingness, Jane's presence gave Barnaby something he'd been sorely missing.

His humanity.

A purpose.

Squeezing his hands together until the knuckles popped, he made a decision. Not only did he vow to keep her safe or perish trying, but also he would destroy Thompson and his hellish corporation. Jane deserved to have her pain vindicated. Those other women deserved to be freed.

The only reason Barnaby hadn't left immediately to take down that sick bastard was because of the woman sleeping in the bed.

He couldn't leave Jane.

What about his Indebted contract, the very thing that drew the danger to Jane?

If he couldn't break his contract, he had to leave her.

Criminy, he wanted one shot, just one, at a future with this woman. But to have a chance, he needed to leave so the minion wouldn't be drawn to her. Then he'd have to try to break his Indebted curse.

He owed her that much.

At the end of the day, a future for them would be her decision, and he'd worry about that if they even survived that far.

For now, all that stood between Jane and the minion's deadly retribution was Barnaby.

• • •

The next week rolled along in a predictable routine. Jane slept more than she ever had in her entire life, and each time she woke up, Barnaby was right there, his handsome face creased into the same heartwarming smile. Which would have been perfect in any situation but this current one.

On the seventh morning, Jane got up on her own, made her own sandwich—thank you very much—and walked on her own steam across the entire cabin to open the door and stand on the porch.

Barnaby's quick forays into the surrounding forest set her nerves on edge. He was never gone more than fifteen minutes at a time, but he always left after he had cocked his head to the side, as if he heard something. Then he'd dash out the door. Just as suddenly, he'd come right back, like nothing had happened.

Only, she could tell by the furrow in his brow, it wasn't nothing.

Of course, earlier in the week, he'd left for less than an hour to pick up "real clothes," as he put it, for her to wear. His friend, Dante, who had helped spring her from the psych ward, had dropped off a box of clothes at a local market for Barnaby to pick up. In the box, she found pants and tops, bras and underwear, and even a cute sundress. His friend had quite the eye for fashion.

When Barnaby began to fidget a few days later, she knew something more occupied his thoughts. He missed her obvious chess feint, and she took his queen without protest. In the fresh air and midmorning light, not even the John Denver tune relaxed him today.

"All right, Barnaby, spill it. What's going on?"

"Nothing." The smile didn't reach his eyes

"Want to try that again?"

"Oh ho, now you're the polygraph test?"

"No, but I'm a decent profiler."

His grave tone chilled her skin. "I know."

"You've started acting differently. Like you need to be somewhere." It dawned on her. "I've overstayed my welcome, haven't I?"

"No!" He hit the table hard enough to make a castle fall, then mumbled, "My apologies. You didn't deserve that tone."

"Barnaby. If there's something you need to do, please don't let me stop you. Heck, if you need me to go somewhere, I'll leave. I appreciate all that you've done for me, but you have a life to live."

Shoving his fingers through his thick brown hair, he grimaced. "That's just it. I only have one little task that will take me away from here for several hours, maybe a day at most."

Her heart drumming in her chest, she rapidly assessed the security limitations of the cabin and an escape route if she had to stay here alone. "No problem. You've earned a break from managing this invalid."

"It's not like that at all."

"Then what?"

"I can't say."

A little ember of pique glowed inside of her, an emotion she hadn't nurtured in a long time. "You can't say? I share an awful experience no human should have to endure, and you can't tell me what's bothering you?"

"It's not that simple," he said from a tight jaw.

"Try me."

"You can't know."

Jane snapped, "Why not?"

"Because it would be dangerous if you knew my secrets."

"Like having someone try to kill me dangerous? I already have the corner on that market."

"No, nothing quite like that." He clamped his mouth shut.

The ember of irritation flickered to flame. An emotion she had long suppressed sparked, here, now, eager to burn.

"So what then?" she snarled. "Let's get real. What could be worse? Because waiting for me back in San Francisco, with a limitless desire for revenge, is my worst-case scenario where the most catastrophic possibility *isn't* death. Not only does that maniac want to breed with me, but also I have no job, no future, and couldn't run away if my life depended on it, because then the DEA would track me down and eliminate me. So do you still believe my life will be in more danger if you tell me what the hell is bugging you? Because by my calculations, it's statistically impossible that your story will make a dent in the amount of crap I'm in."

"Please, Jane." He glanced at his hand. "Bloody hell."

With zero effort, he'd smashed the king between his thumb and forefinger.

The pieces were solid ivory.

His eyes had gone from blue to a dangerous black.

She gulped and nodded at the pulverized chess piece. "Does your secret have anything to do with the strength you hide from me? The unnatural speed? Or your bogus accent that slips every so often?"

"I don't know about—"

"How about the way your eyes turn colors? Or that you're on edge 90 percent of the time?"

"Please."

"Please what? Please accept your explanation? Done." Her hand shook as she waved it over the board. "Now, out with it."

"God's teeth, Jane. You have no idea. None." The way he spat the words, like he dragged them out of his soul, chilled her blood. Like he despised her for making him say the words.

"I've seen just about everything."

"You. I can't—"

"Barnaby," she cut off his stammering. "What have you said time and again?"

"What?"

"You keep saying 'trust me.' Tell you what: you want my trust, maybe you should start with some effort on your side of the table."

"Jane." With a defeated huff of air, he dropped his face into his hands. "Shite. You will be the death of me."

His eyes had lightened back to blue, and sadness floated over his face. Then he stared at her until holding his gaze became uncomfortable.

"Well, here goes." Tapping an uninjured pawn on the board, he looked up at the ceiling for what seemed like an eternity. "So I'm pretty old."

"What, like, thirty?"

His barked laugh held no happiness. "Much older than that. Try over 400 years old."

A bubble of insane laughter rose up like carbonation. "You can't be serious?"

His steady stare answered her question. "Is this your story or mine?"

She wanted the truth. Careful what she wished for. "Oh my God, you're serious." She swallowed. "How?"

He nodded. "So. I was born in 1532, the year of our Lord, in London, England. Over the years, my family had ascended into the peerage through a combination of serendipity and machinations. Once my twin brother and I reached our majority, we were sent to court, as one does."

"Twin?"

"Not so glamorous, considering that we were the fifth and sixth sons, respectively. Very poor prospects in those days. So yes, we were sent to court."

"Court?"

"The court of Elizabeth, Queen of England. Gloriana." His rapt expression held more than reverence.

She paused a full ten seconds, assessing whether she was having an LSD flashback. Nope. Solid ground under her. Furniture didn't turn into animals.

"What. The. Hell."

"'S'true, Jane. Listen to the words. Listen for the truth. You can hear it."

Earnest, straightforward. No stumbling over words or tightening vowels. Good grief. This couldn't actually be true.

Could it?

He reached out his hand, then curled it into a fist. "Hear me out. All of it. Then you can pass judgment." Sincerity, not insanity, shone from his eyes.

"I asked for it. All right, then." She tamped down irritation. "You knew Queen Elizabeth of England?"

"Yes."

"What was she like?" She was actually going along with this tale.

"Ah, Bess, she was bonny and shrewd, and I so adored her."

"Wait. How well did you know Queen Elizabeth?"

"I more than knew her." He winked. "We were lovers."

"What?"

"You see, my brother happened upon an idea—a stroke of genius that kept us flush with free time. We split our duties as Master of the Horse. Because we were newcomers, few knew that we were twins. Fewer still knew that both of us came to court. So I would serve for a week, and my brother, Robert Dudley, would serve a week. And so it went, each week playing at being Robert. When I wasn't at court, I went by the name Barnaby Emerson and remained discreetly hidden. For a time, life moved along in a comfortable routine."

"Until?"

"Until I fell madly in love with my queen. How I loved the glints of golden fire in her fierce gaze. Those were halcyon days. We were awash with love, invincible, with an exciting future ahead of us. Only, there were those who wanted her dead. She had radical ideas about the Church of England that ran contrary to all that the Catholics held dear. One attempt on her life nearly succeeded. She'd been poisoned. As I lay with her in my arms as she frothed and struggled to breathe, I called out to the heavens for help. Anything to save my dear Bess."

Lines of sadness furrowed his brow, and Jane believed the emotion. But not the story. However, she'd give him until the end of his "explanation," as promised.

"There is more you should know." He pressed his mouth into a thin line, then finally blinked and relaxed. "Bess carried and bore my child."

"No. She never had a baby."

"It was kept secret, but yes, she most certainly did have a child. I know. I put it there. You can imagine the fear when my pregnant love lay at death's door. When I called to the heavens above for help, someone answered my plea. Something, I should say."

Fine. She would play along. "God?"

"Quite the opposite. The human form of Satan on this Earth."

"I don't understand."

"A creature named Jerahmeel, whose only purpose in this world is to trick people into selling their souls to him, where they will live an unnaturally long life and serve his evil appetite."

"You sold your soul?"

"When Jerahmeel answered my call, he promised to save my Bess if I would but sign a small contract. I signed, she lived and bore my daughter in secret, and all was good ... until Jerahmeel showed up again, demanding payment."

"What did you pay?"

"Bess, my brother, my daughter, my life. Everything. I left it all behind and became an Indebted, a hired killer, collecting evil souls to feed Jerahmeel."

Nothing in his speech patterns indicated deception.

After all those acid trips, Jane probably deserved for this story to be true.

Chapter 15

After a moment's hesitation where he swallowed a lump of shame, he lifted his pants leg. "I kill with this blade." The damn thing gave off a green glow.

She gasped. "It's ...?"

"Cursed? Yes, along with me. Due to the knife's call, there will come a point where I can no longer resist the urge to kill a criminal. Jerahmeel, through the blade, forces me to track down and destroy dark souls. The knife leads me to the worst criminals."

"Well, that makes murder a-okay then, right?" The ocean blue of her eyes turned flat, suspicious, and her disbelief cut him more surely than any metal weapon ever could.

He struggled to recover. "No, you don't understand. It's not bad enough that I have to kill. What scares me is that at some point, I'll have to leave you to perform my ... job. I won't have a choice. That's when you'll be most vulnerable."

"I'm sure I'll manage." The brave face she mustered scared him more than her fear.

"It gets worse. If Jerahmeel finds out I have an attachment to any human, he will try to interfere, if only to keep me focused on doing his work."

"Interfere?"

"Destroy you." He let the words drop like two bricks.

"Oh."

"Yes. Oh."

"But you will live for hundreds more years?"

He hesitated. "Yes."

She pressed her lips into an unhappy line. "So a long-term relationship for you is really long term, then?"

"What?"

Anger glinting in her fierce expression shifted into a ghost of a smile. "Well, damn it all. Isn't this just fabulous?"

"Come again?" The hard set to her jaw worried him.

A wry lift to the corner of her mouth gave him a flicker of hope. "How perfect are we? I should be declared insane. You've got a story that will seal my commitment to the asylum if I ever tell it. Perfect."

"You're not horrified?"

Her high-pitched laugh came out weak, strained. "Yeah, I'm pretty creeped out right now. It's not every day I hang out with a cold-blooded killer. Hold on, that's not true if you count the past year of my life. Could be the company I'm keeping."

When he shifted, she flinched, and he cursed himself all over again.

"I won't hurt you, I swear." He wanted to touch her, convince her of his sincerity, make her forget the horrors she'd survived. Make her forget the horror that he represented.

"You won't hurt me? Ha. See, that's the only part of this cock-and-bull story that I completely believe." She dropped her head into her hands.

"It's true." He studied her hunched shoulders. "Why aren't you running away from me?"

She propped her chin on her fisted hand. "First, I can't get away. Not yet. Second, you are judged by your actions, not your history."

"Pardon?"

"We both have pasts that are better left hidden." She held up a hand at his protest. "So, in Saigon, were you Indebted then?"

"Yes."

"What were you doing there?"

"Getting easy kills." In for a penny. "And trying to find an ancient text rumored to have the knowledge to free me from this life."

Her amazed expression opened like the petals of a flower. "Really? You were trying to stop being what you are?"

"Wouldn't you?"

"Well ... yeah, probably." She shook her head. "So you had extra strength then?"

"Yes, part of my curse means that it's particularly hard for me to be killed, which is a bonus in a war zone."

"Makes sense. So why did you stay with me in the closet? Why didn't you attack that guy and take him out? Or escape?"

"Because I couldn't risk you being hurt."

She bit her lower lip. "What about that promise on the roof to find me?"

"I failed. If I hadn't done what I promised, you might not have suffered."

"I'm sure you had your own life to lead."

"You truly want to know what I was doing between Saigon and now?"

"Yes."

"Nothing, all right?" he spat. "I was doing nothing except killing criminals because I'm not strong enough to resist the knife's call. I have nothing to show for the past six years."

Turning her palms up, she said, "It's not your job to save me, Barnaby."

"By the gods above, it is, when I'm the cause of your danger." He consciously relaxed his fisted hands when she scooted back. "A true man keeps his promise. There's no way I can atone for what happened to you. Even if we had a future ..."

"Even if we had a future, it's gone now, right?" Pointing to her chest, she added, "Because we can't ... because ... yeah."

"No! That's not what I mean."

She wrapped her hands over each upper arm. "Don't lie on my account. I know the score. I know what's happened to me. I'm not fit for anyone's future."

"That's not what I'm saying at all." How had he lost all control of this conversation? She wasn't the problem. Not even close.

"Bull."

"Please."

Between her tear-filled eyes and the pulse pounding at her neck, he didn't know how to help. A red flush crept over her neck, and she laced her fingers together, as if by doing so she could hold herself together.

Her chin rose. "Look, I'd love to storm out and go for a long walk to process all this craziness, but my stupid legs aren't working enough to get more than fifty feet into the wilderness on account of fallout from my bad workplace decisions, the miscarriage of a cult leader's baby, and forced tranquilizer use. So I'm going to have to ask you to leave me alone for a while."

"Jane ..."

"You say you're jonesing for a kill. Why don't you go get it?" The ice in her voice chilled his skin.

"What?"

"Put your money where your mouth is. Get out. Please."

"Does it count that this is my cabin?"

Like a vase shattering, she burst into tears.

Coward that he was, Barnaby fled.

• • •

Jane's wretched day only got worse when night started to fall and there was no sign of Barnaby.

Since she had used up her quota of walking by pacing, she now lolled on the couch in her ill-fitting tracksuit, exhausted. Way too many trips to the front window and back, combined with her battered heart, had left her spent in body and spirit.

Oh my God, she'd kicked Barnaby out of his own house. Told him to go and do the thing that disturbed her most about him.

Why was she scared? He'd never hurt her, right?

So what if he'd sacrificed his entire existence years ago to save flippin' Elizabeth, Queen of England. Maybe he could get sainthood.

Sure, he had protected Jane in Saigon, and then he'd rescued her from the hellish psych ward.

Then he upended his entire life and helped her to heal, waiting on her hand and foot, and allowing her to regain her strength.

She wasn't scared of Barnaby.

Jane was scared of herself, scared that she might never deserve a life with a good man. A man who put others ahead of himself.

Nasty self-contempt rattled against her ribs.

God, look what she'd done, in the name of her job.

What right did she have to judge him?

The crunch of gravel and the flash of headlights made her heart jump in her chest.

She steeled herself to give Barnaby the apology he deserved.

A car door slammed.

All right. She took a deep breath.

Then a second door slammed, and a third.

At the fourth door slam, fear drove her to her feet next to the couch.

Male voices filtered through the walls.

A shadow flickered across the front window, followed by a harsh flashlight beam that pierced the interior of the cabin.

She dove to the floor.

Maybe it was the police?

Maybe monkeys would fly out of her butt.

At a rap on the door, she jumped.

"... said she'd be in here," a male voice growled.

A more tenor-voiced man replied, "The girl at the store said he drove off by himself ... your woman's got to be in the cabin."

"Then get in there and find her."

"We don't know she's here for sure. It's breaking and entering."

"Like I care about that shit? I want her ass here. Now. Dig it?" She knew that growling voice. Sweat beaded her upper lip.

"Roger, boss."

At the first heavy thud against the door, she scanned the cabin for an escape route.

One way in and out through the front door, unless she counted the porch. Suspended at least twenty feet above the steep mountainside below, the porch wouldn't work. Too weak to climb down the angled cantilevered supports and drop to the ground, she had run out of options in record time.

The thuds stopped.

She crawled to the bedroom.

How about the small closet? No. Someone would look there for sure. Her only chance was to convince them no one was home.

A crash of glass from the front window sent shards of dread slicing through her nerves.

Dragging herself under the bed, she edged toward the wall as footsteps came closer. She curled into a ball, hugging her knees to her chest.

The overhead light came on.

With a familiar clomp, a pair of tan Dingos scuffed to a halt at the end of the bed.

A second set of shoes, worn loafers, stopped about four feet away from Jane, next to the chair Barnaby sat in while she slept. Her heart rate cranked into high gear.

"Jesus, when I get my hands on that woman, she'll be sorry, that's all I can say."

Thumps and crashes from the kitchen and living room bore testament to the destruction of Barnaby's cabin retreat. Somehow, she'd pay for the damage. Only right, since Thompson and his buddies would never have come here if it weren't for Jane and her failed mission.

God, how she'd failed.

The loafers pivoted ninety degrees away from her hiding place.

Then the bedside lamp shattered, tiny pieces of glass skidding under the bed.

With a crunch on the ruined material, the loafers moved away.

Silence.

Maybe they'd left.

Out of the corner of her eye, the buckles on the damned Dingo boots glinted as they came to a stop on the other side of the bed.

Sweat dripped down her forehead, and she bit her fist to keep quiet.

"Hello, lost little dove." Thompson's voice vibrated with barely contained fury.

Before she could turn, her head jerked as Thompson dragged her by her hair from under the bed. Glass scored her arms. Pain blasted from her scalp as he pulled her to a sitting position.

"Get up," Thompson said in a too-calm-to-be-believed tone.

His heavy, sweaty face looming over her. Same man, same cruelty.

On tottering legs, she stood up against the closet door, using the handle for support.

Dusty loafers, that other jerk, chuckled from behind Thompson's shoulder.

Two other men hovered in the doorway of the bedroom.

The DEA did not have a training module for this scenario.

Because there was no solution.

A strange calm settled over Jane. All her struggle to find a purpose in this crazy world. It had all been for nothing.

Poor Barnaby. He'd rescued her only to postpone the inevitable outcome.

A metal click grabbed her attention. Thompson pointed a black Magnum at her.

Well, this was going to hurt.

Her legs shook. They wouldn't hold her for long.

Probably didn't need much time anyway. Still, a perverse instinct to stall the unavoidable took over.

"Why are you doing this, Thompson?" she asked.

"You know too much." He licked those damp lips that previously had been all over her.

She shuddered. "No one would believe me, with as many drugs as were in my system. So why all the trouble?"

"Who wants to take a chance with a narc?"

"I'm not—"

"Shut up. Your boss, Howard, and I are business partners. I know what you are."

Confirmation of her fears nailed her between the eyes. "Please, I—"

"Don't care. You're done." He motioned dusty loafers over and handed him the gun. "Actually, you do it. I don't want any blood on my hands."

"What harm could another drop do?" Devil made her ask. She had a serious case of the don't-cares.

Thompson snatched the gun back himself and leveled it at her head.

The world exploded.

CHAPTER 16

Barnaby dragged his sorry ass back to Jane, steering the car back to the cabin.

His entire existence. For nothing. And the relief he felt from that kill earlier today, like it somehow gave his life purpose? Bunk and hypocrisy.

The only thing preventing his separation from humanity waited in that cabin.

His instinct for danger went off the charts, nearly blinding him.

Fifty yards before cresting the top of the mountain, he stomped the brakes and parked the Nova. Leaving the door open, he disappeared into the woods and slunk his way to the cabin. With the sun down, the darkness allowed him to get within twenty feet of the front door.

A dark Chrysler Imperial hissed and popped in front of the closed cabin door. Where the living room window had been, now jagged pieces of broken glass jutted up from the sill. Voices and thuds from within the cabin iced Barnaby's blood.

Jane.

As he crouched and sidled to the window, the voices confirmed his worst fears.

"Why are you doing this, Thompson?" Her voice, thin in the night air, drove Barnaby to a protective madness.

When he peered through the ruined window, light from the bedroom cast two men in shadows. But the voices came from within that room.

The minion.

And Jane.

Barnaby heard a metallic click that stopped his heart.

With one smooth movement, he drew the knife from his leg sheath and hurdled the windowsill. In two steps, he'd reached the men in the doorway and felled them with lightning-fast thrusts of the knife.

Before the men could drop, Barnaby sunk the blade into the chest of a big, hulking man several feet away from Thompson.

Pivoting, Barnaby spied Jane's mouth opening in an O of horror as Thompson aimed a gun squarely at her. She clutched the closet doorknob in a white-knuckled grip.

"Don't move," the man snarled.

Thompson could have been talking to either of them, but Barnaby held still, just in case. The distance to save Jane from a bullet was too great. The bed and a minion stood in the way. Barnaby could vault the bed but would never stop Thompson in time.

But if the minion fired and missed, that would give Barnaby enough time to get to Thompson.

Locking his gaze on to Jane, Barnaby mouthed the word "down." When Thompson spun back to him, Barnaby held stock-still.

"I will not have my empire destroyed by lowlifes like you two," Thompson seethed. His eyes darted over the bodies of his fallen comrades, and he wiped sweat from his forehead. "I won't fail my master, either."

"We won't tell," Barnaby said.

Thompson's wild, minion-insane eyes rolled in his sockets. "Don't care what you will and won't do, Indebted. I'm removing your options. Besides, lord Jerahmeel requires my obedience. Therefore, if I cannot mate with her, then she will die."

Barnaby hurled himself at the man.

Thompson pulled the trigger.

Jane dropped to the floor, limp.

Thompson nailed Barnaby in the head with the butt of the gun, staggering him backward. Barnaby shook his head and planted his feet, ready to strike, but his hands were empty.

The knife lay on the floor, inches from Jane.

As she lifted her head and reached for the knife, Barnaby howled a warning to stop. Any mortal who touched the blade would die instantly.

Recoiling as if a snake had bitten her, Jane curled into a ball as Thompson took aim at her again.

Barnaby hit the man square between the shoulder blades, and the gun went off in a splinter of wood inches from her head. Jane yelped. God, if she'd been hit ... Barnaby leveled Thompson with a few good blows and a cracking kick to the shin. Then Thompson planted his meaty fist into Barnaby's cheekbone, enough to make stars spin around Barnaby's head. Whoreson minion was tremendously strong.

Thompson cocked the gun again. "All right, you first, Mr. Hero. I'll take my time finishing off Ms. Rat afterward."

Not acceptable. Barnaby drove Thompson into the far wall, indenting the solid wood wall and knocking the gun out of the man's hand. The desire to reconnect with the cursed knife drove Barnaby insane. He wanted to kill the minion, but he needed to have the knife in his hand when he did it. Separation from the knife tore Barnaby apart.

In the split second he turned his back on Thompson, the minion pounded Barnaby in a commendable set of kidney punches. Barnaby would piss blood later. If there was a later. He hauled air into his lungs and braced for another impact when he felt the man loom over him. Barnaby couldn't discern much with his swollen eyes and addled brain.

Then, a bang and thud.

Then nothing.

Because he didn't know what he would find, Barnaby raised his head slowly, praying that the gunshot had missed Jane.

Her tear-streaked face and wide, teal eyes smashed his heart to pieces. Thompson lay gasping on the cabin floor, a spreading bloom of blood soaking his shirt. Jane's hand shook, but she kept the gun aimed at Thompson.

Then the damned minion planted his meaty hands on the floor and pushed to a sitting position.

He was getting up.

And his furious gaze had locked on to Jane.

No. Barnaby grabbed his knife and plunged it into Thompson's chest, right below the sternum. The knife flared as it drank the corrupt soul into the metal. Barnaby sighed in blissful relief.

At a strangled cry from Jane, though, his joy at the kill drained into the floor to mingle with Thompson's blood.

"Oh, my love," he said softly. Easing the gun out of her grip, he set it far away from the now-still body on the floor. Quickly, he cleaned and stowed his knife.

"Barnaby? You came back." When her voice cracked like that, his heart flipped over.

He pulled her into his arms and held on until she squeaked in pain. His grip was too tight. Couldn't help it. This was Jane. He'd nearly lost her because of his pride. She was his last anchor to humanity.

Without her, he would be a husk of a man. A sham of a living creature.

He brushed his mouth over her forehead, almost to convince himself that she lived. Her skin, clean and vital, reassured him.

"Oh my God, those men—Thompson—was going to kill me. What happened to Thompson? He looked bigger, meaner ... possessed, almost," she said. "You killed them so quickly? With that knife?"

Leaning back, he blew out air he didn't know he'd been holding. "I'm sorry you had to see that."

"You really are a killer, aren't you? That whole story was completely true."

"I wouldn't lie to you."

She pushed a fall of hair off of her face. "Well, I'm a killer now, too."

"It's not the same. What you had to do was different."

Her voice registered as barely a whisper. "I killed him."

"He would have hurt you, Jane. Besides, you only slowed Thompson down so I could finish him off."

Staring at her shaking hands, she said, "It's still a crime."

"No. It's self-defense. Truly." How refreshing to see someone care about their kill. Barnaby had lost that sensitivity a hundred or so years ago. "Let's get out of this room," he said, helping her step over the two bodies in the bedroom doorway.

He deposited her on the couch, knowing he should clean up the cabin and dispose of the bodies. But he couldn't do it right away. He couldn't let go of her.

That damned knife warmed his leg in sated satisfaction, almost taunting him.

Because the reason Barnaby hadn't been here to protect her would be an issue until the end of time.

Which was more important? Feeding the incredible knife lust and retaining near-immortal status?

Or Jane.

After dropping a kiss square on her soft lips, he stroked her long, tangled hair. What would life be like, spending every day with her in his arms?

Damned amazing, to be honest.

He eased her away from him with another kiss and worked on setting the cabin to rights. When he moved the bodies, lifting each one like it weighed nothing, the horror in her eyes indicted him more than any uttered phrase ever could.

A monster. He'd become a monster.

Hours later, as false dawn made the sky glow, Barnaby had removed all traces of blood and glass. He'd run the Chrysler off a cliff and scattered the bodies all around. Hopefully carrion birds would take care of the evidence well before anyone discovered the dead men.

All that remained was to replace the window, and the cabin would be back to normal.

Only, truth be told, he never wanted to come back here.

This cabin represented his attempts to escape his empty existence. This place represented where he nearly lost what he held most dear in this world.

God willing, this cabin would soon be part of Barnaby's distant past.

Slumping into the couch cushion, he leaned back.

"Are you okay?" Jane asked.

"You're alive, so yes."

"Yes, well ..."

So he went for levity. Anything to smooth the furrows from her brow. "Hey, great shooting, by the way."

"Thank goodness they taught us women *some* useful skills." Her tiny smile gave him hope.

"You were perfect. I'm only sorry I wasn't here before Thompson found you."

"You had to go. Your job." She held up her hand. "Look, it's okay. I understand that some things are out of your control. Lord knows, I get that."

Pushing back to his feet, he paced. "I want to try for a future with you, but not as the creature I am right now."

"I don't understand."

A caged animal. He'd become trapped between what he wanted most in this world and the monster he had become. He pivoted and stared at her. "I can't live like this anymore."

Even in the early morning light, he couldn't miss how her cheeks paled.

"Live like what?" she said.

"Jane, I ... need to collect my thoughts."

"What?" she whispered, wrapping thin arms around her legs.

He'd do anything to remove the stark fear on her lovely face.

Anything?

The answer whispered, like a gossamer thought floating just out of reach.

What did his instincts tell him? His traitorous sixth sense had gone to sleep.

No help there.

A new kind of panic, different from what he'd felt since finding Jane, grabbed hold of him and didn't let go. He couldn't breathe.

"I'm sorry. I, um, need a little space."

The downturn of her lips hurt more than anything he'd felt in four centuries. But he had to get his head screwed on straight.

"You need space?" Her flat voice drifted in a hopeless, gray tone.

He reached out, then dropped his hand. "It's not like that."

"It never is, Barnaby." Her lips pressed into a sad, straight line.

"No, Jane, it's not what you think."

"You presume to know how I think?" She didn't meet his eyes but stared somewhere over his shoulder. "Go. Get your space."

"Jane—"

"Go."

He walked to the table, looked straight at her, deliberately placed his car keys on the table, and strode out of the cabin.

CHAPTER 17

Like an idiot, she'd sent Barnaby packing. Again. Apparently, she couldn't learn.

How did things turn out the last time you made him leave?

Beyond disastrous.

What about his safety, though? Maybe she could find him and make certain that he was okay.

He was a supernatural immortal being. He didn't need her help.

What *did* he need from her?

Absolutely nothing.

The sun rose and lit up the cabin in a cheery glow that taunted her melancholy mood.

Several times, Jane scooped up those damned keys and opened up the front door, ready to drive away. He'd given her a clear choice.

Could she accept Barnaby, an unnatural being?

She had no right to judge.

Real question was, could he accept a broken person like Jane?

Afternoon crawled into evening. Restless, she couldn't sleep, couldn't get comfortable.

The problem had less to do with the man who exited the cabin and more to do with the woman remaining inside.

I can't live like this anymore, he'd said.

Cold fingers of fear slid over her neck and squeezed.

I can't live like this anymore.

How far would he go to fulfill that promise?

Twilight darkened the skies, and she shivered in the light breeze through the broken window. She'd long since stopped jumping at each tiny noise outside.

Who cared? The man she loved, her calm in the storm, the man who had challenged the devil's own henchman to save her life, had left.

She sniffed. Nope, tears had long since dried up. She had nothing left but a sucking emptiness that started out small and expanded until it wormed its way through her entire chest.

How could he have done this?

To her, the little voice in her head whispered.

How selfish could she be? He left.

Because she told him to.

What the heck did she expect?

God, she wanted Barnaby back, cursed existence and all. She wanted his jaunty smile and twinkling blue eyes. What she'd give to feel his muscled arms around her again.

She peered out the window into the moonlit night.

Like he'd never existed, Barnaby was gone.

The cruelty of the entire situation hit her like a truck plowing her over. She sagged against the porch door frame. Her entire soul had been ripped in half.

Her anchor. Gone.

Her sanity, following.

• • •

The next morning dawned cool, bright, and cheery, much to Jane's disgust. Her sleep had been horrendous, partly due to the open window allowing chilly air to move unimpeded through the house. And partly due to ... yeah.

Shaking her arms and legs to warm up, she shuffled into the kitchen. Even with a spoon, bowl, powdered milk, and a cornflakes box laid out on the counter, she couldn't pull it off. She kept staring at the items, not certain what to do.

So instead, she sank to the floor with a death grip on the spoon.

He hadn't returned.

Well, there you had it.

She couldn't stay here. Eventually, someone would figure out that Thompson's crew had disappeared near Santa Cruz. They would eventually find Barnaby's cabin. Which would lead a curiosity seeker directly to Jane and a whole lot of things she couldn't explain.

The spoon clutched in her hand blurred into the image of Barnaby's smiling face. She squeezed her eyes closed and rubbed her eyes with the other hand, trying something—anything—to remove him from her memory. It didn't work.

When her head lolled back on the cabinet and she finally opened her eyes, darned if she didn't see his face again. She blinked hard. It didn't help. She gripped the spoon harder, as if doing so would bolster her sanity.

Even now, she could swear the muscles of his arms flexed and his chest rose with a sigh. She even saw the corner of his strong mouth rise in a wry smile.

With every nuance of behavior in her imagined vision, the vice around her heart cranked down tighter and tighter.

"Jane."

Oh great, now she was hallucinating sounds. Maybe the LSD from the People's Palace had come back to haunt her.

Maybe Barnaby haunted her.

The burn in her chest amplified when she blinked and he didn't disappear.

"Jane. I'm here."

"No, you're not." The metal utensil dug into the skin of her palm.

Even though he smiled in the usual Barnaby manner, sadness creased lines on his face.

When he knelt down and touched her on the arm, she yelped. It felt too real, too immediate, too painful.

"It's really me."

"No, it's not."

"Jane." His mellow voice broke her heart. "Do you trust me?"

The imaginary vice loosened half a turn.

He had come back.

"I trust you, Barnaby."

She buried her head on bent knees.

"Where did you go?"

"I never left. Not really." He sank down to sit near her on the floor. "Z'wounds, Jane. I couldn't leave you."

Snapping her head up to stare at him, she said, "What?"

He took her free hand in his big, rough one, turned her palm up, and dropped a gentle kiss onto her wrist.

The screws on the vice around her heart unwound with each swipe of his lips on her skin. As the pressure eased up in her chest, the emptiness faded. She relaxed her grip on the spoon but couldn't let it go yet.

"You're really here," she whispered.

"You bet I am." The light in his eyes returned, along with ... fear? "So, Jane?"

"Yes."

"I was always in sight of this cabin. Every time I tried to go farther away, you were like a magnet, pulling me back." He shoved a hand through his hair. "Do you even understand what I'm trying to say? I couldn't leave you if I tried."

"I understand."

"Really?" His boyish grin made her toes tingle.

"Yeah. For real. I tried to leave several times, but couldn't."

"Truth?"

"Truth."

His eyes shone. "In four centuries roaming this earth, I have never loved a woman the way I love you, Jane." He swallowed. "I have no right to ask. I'm a monster. Criminy, I have no right—"

When she pressed her finger to his lips, he froze in place, gripping her wrist like a lifeline.

"I have no right, either, Barnaby. Neither of us is a whole person."

"Maybe we can be whole together." He rubbed his chin. "God's teeth, I'll beg if necessary."

Her heart pounded. "No, you don't—"

His grip on her hand ached, but she wouldn't make him let go for a million dollars.

In the early morning light, his eyes shone, and the big man opened his mouth to speak twice before getting the words out. "We have no guarantees. As long as I'm Indebted, you will be in danger. And if you're with me, your normal human life is gone. We have to hide."

"I'm good at hiding." She studied the handsome sweep of his hair over his forehead. "Do you really want out of your contract?"

"Yes. But I don't even know if it's possible."

"Then I want to help you try. And no, I don't care about being in danger. I'm getting pretty good at it."

His blue eyes lit up, and his brows rose. "Could we try?"

"There's nothing I want more than to be with you for whatever forever means for us. We'll go find those scrolls in Vietnam."

"When travel is safe."

"But soon. Together." She twined her fingers in his. "Before we go back to Vietnam, would you help me free those women and expose the People's Palace?"

"After what you endured? It would be my pleasure."

"Then we'll go make you human again."

"I don't know if it can be done. Or if I would survive. If you object, I won't do it. I can stay Indebted and use my power to keep you safe from any new minions Jerahmeel sends."

A cold chill ran down her spine. "What do you want, Barnaby?"

Pulling her hand up, he brushed his lips across her knuckles. "I want to become a real man for you. Only you, Jane."

"Then that's what you should do."

He pulled her close and kissed her. She returned it with interest, pouring her love for him into the contact.

When he leaned back, he ran his index finger down her cheek until she shivered.

"One question, sweetling," he said.

"Yes?"

"Could I have that spoon back? You're going to strangle it."

She hiccupped a sob and laughed. "Of course." She loosened her grip until he gently extricated the utensil, but the lack of something to hold on to made her heart patter.

Until she focused on Barnaby.

She had anchored him to this world.

And he was her anchor.

Acknowledgments

Thank you to the indomitable Gwen Hayes, who graciously turned this manuscript around in record time, complete with her fabulous feedback. I also appreciate Crimson Romance editor Julie Sturgeon's amazing edits, always spot-on and continually pushing me to make these books so much better.

Thanks to hubby, who is ever eager to provide character name suggestions ("Buck Naked") and title possibilities ("Flame Gone Out Then Exploding Again"). For a guy who has no clue about the romance genre, he's really ... not very helpful. But he's supportive, and that's fine.

Finally, as I conclude this series and the journey while writing it, the last thank you goes to my patients. Their trust as they allow me to travel with them through their pain, joy, fear, hope, death, and life is what has created the rich texture in the stories. Without my patients, there would be no writing.

Author's Notes

The Tet Offensive (phase I) began late on January 30, 1968. Numerous surprise attacks occurred on that date up and down the Ho Chi Minh trail and reaching into Saigon. These attacks continued through March of 1968. This campaign was a major turning point for the entire Vietnam War. U.S. losses tallied at approximately 4,000 troops killed and 20,000 wounded during this time period.

While the U.S. Embassy in then Saigon (now Ho Chi Minh City) did have an incursion made into its outer walls by the Vietcong during the Tet Offensive, military police repelled and killed the small invading force. In this story, I took liberties with the extent to which the embassy was breached. Also, to my knowledge, there were no helicopter transports that night. However, I'm always haunted by Dutch photographer Hubert van Es's iconic photo taken on the final day in Saigon right before the city finally fell to the North Vietnamese in 1975. It's that image I had in my mind when I wrote the helicopter-roof scene. Then I added the big explosion, which is an acknowledged embellishment.

The People's Palace and Tim Thompson are modeled very loosely on the People's Temple and leader, Jim Jones. As you recall, Jim Jones's cult moved down to South America, mixed up some Kool-Aid, and from there, things went poorly for everyone involved.

The music referenced in this novella is from the Billboard charts late in 1967/1968 and in 1973/1974, though a few songs may have technically been released after the events of the story.

Last but not least, if you are a TV Land junkie/nerd, you'll have called me out on the timing of the *The Bionic Woman* reference. I know. The Bionic Woman (who is way more awesome than the Six Million Dollar Man, IMHO) debuted as a partner for Steve Austin in 1975. So yes, a year premature on the mention, but come on now, Lindsay Wagner was awesome in those tracksuits. I couldn't resist the reference!

Thank you for picking up a copy of my book. It's readers like you who encourage writers to keep creating new worlds. Would you please consider leaving a review at your bookseller or Goodreads? Better yet, tell someone else about the book. And of course, readers are always welcome to provide feedback or ask questions here: *jillian@jilliandavid.net*

Playlist

For readers who like to cue up the music before reading, here's the playlist for this novella. I hope you enjoy listening to these songs as much as I did! These tunes totally put me in the 1968/1974 mood ...

Jackie Wilson "Higher and Higher"
Herman's Hermits "There's a Kind of Hush All Over the World"
The Monkees "Daydream Believer"
The 5th Dimension "Up, Up and Away"
Santana "Evil Ways"
Jimi Hendrix "Machine Gun"
Blue Swede "Hooked on a Feeling"
The Carpenters "Top of the World"
Kool & the Gang "Jungle Boogie"
Elton John "Don't Let the Sun Go Down on Me"
Bachman-Turner Overdrive "Takin' Care of Business"
Grand Funk Railroad "The Loco-Motion"
Jim Croce "Time in a Bottle"
John Denver "Sunshine on My Shoulders"

While editing this novella, I had Melanie's "Lay Down (Candles in the Rain)" on eternal repeat.

More from This Author
Flame Unleashed by Jillian David

Holy hell, she needed to kill someone.

Impractical stiletto leather boots snapped against concrete as she strode up the chipped sidewalk near the Warehouse District of New Orleans. Dilapidated, abandoned buildings clashed with garish bars that depended on sports fans, college students, and tourists. This section of Port Street wasn't a main road or a well-to-do area of town. Good. That meant fewer tourists but more denizens like her—beings that worked best in the shadows.

Tonight, there must have been a football game or another equally inane reason to imbibe, judging from the amount of people out. Of course, drunkenness was not a crime, despite what she might think of her former husband, God rest his bastard soul. No matter, she would find some kind of louse among the lushes before this night ended.

Farther down the street, the quality of the architecture deteriorated. Dozens of motorcycles were parked outside one raucous establishment. No peppy zydeco tunes here. Instead, tired metal beats drifted into the street. Yes, this area would do nicely for her evening's goals.

Just another night in a city, obtaining her requisite kills. The macabre had become routine. How sad.

A few men leaned against the cinderblock storefront, faint light illuminating the tips of their cigarettes. When she sauntered by, paused, and pretended to contemplate entering the bar, she had their attention. Let them take note, lulled into a sense of security.

Enjoy the view while you can, boys.

One man caught her knife's interest—the blade craved criminals. What remained of the man's bone-straight hair had been pulled into a thin ponytail, and a leather vest strained over his belly. Its fringe was overkill, along with silver detailing that glinted on the new motorcycle boots. He probably owned one of those souped-up custom Harleys parked front and center.

Leather-clad motorcycle guys were generally sexy, but not tonight's fare. Too bad.

Despite his ridiculous getup, her knife began to pulse on her leg, begging for her to reach into the slit on her leather pants, slide the knife from the sheath beneath her boot, and shove it into …

Got a criminal. Now to reel him in. Might even get the Meaningful Kill tonight.

Tossing her fake hair back off her shoulders, she reveled in the waist-length blond waves. She rarely wore her natural hair down, so this wig brought her to a whole different state of being. Part of her costume was designed to attract certain types of criminals. Part of the costume freed her spirit. So long, mild-mannered nurse. Welcome back, Ms. Blond Bombshell.

Hell, if she had to spend eternity killing criminals, she might as well look good doing it. She had read all the popular books. Who didn't love a sexy demon-slaying chick?

Beside the victims, of course.

She caught the man's eye and licked her lips, a deliberate act that would have been socially unacceptable in her previous life. But this evening's wardrobe veered away from the taffeta, crinoline, and hoops of antebellum evening soirees. Even her torso confined by the black bustier felt like freedom tonight. In a disguise, she could become any woman. The better the disguise, the faster she could forget her real self.

Cursed to kill for hundreds of years as an Indebted, at least she could dictate her attire and the method of carrying out her job. Small victory, but it provided a modicum of control.

When his friend nudged him, the balding man drained his can of beer, crushed it against the wall, and dropped the crumpled metal on the concrete. Despite his nonchalant stance, the glint in his narrow eyes gave away his lust.

He pushed away from the wall. "What's a honey like you doing down here?" His voice sounded like nasally gravel and instantly grated on her nerves.

"Seeing if there's any action."

She glanced at his groin and raised an eyebrow. His Adam's apple bobbed once, twice. With the heels, she topped him by several inches, so his line of sight naturally came to rest on her ample bosom.

Keep looking, nasty guy. It'll be the last thing you see before this night is over.

"What'd you have in mind, beautiful?" His voice oozed over her like sewage slime.

"Let's see where the night takes us." Trailing a hand over her hip, she drew his attention, just like the demon-stalking heroines in the popular novels. Ironic, really, if one considered who was the true demon here.

"I do like a woman who knows what she wants," he drawled, adjusting his jeans.

"Try to keep up ..."

"Right behind you, babe."

Babe. Yuck. Anything but "babe."

She strolled away, giving the man time to contemplate her leather-clad backside. He couldn't help himself. Her heart pounded in anticipation as she led him down the street for a few minutes in search of a location far enough away from the bar. Spying an open gate between two dilapidated buildings, she slipped in ahead of him, giving her backside enough of a wiggle to complete the seduction.

Summoning her best thespian skills, she acted delicate and wilted but still enticing while she leaned against the cement wall inside the abandoned building's courtyard. The man took the bait and boldly placed one hand on the wall next to her head.

As he leaned forward, she tilted her head away. "What's your name, big guy?"

He wetted his lips and leered. "Decker."

She trailed a finger down his chest. "All right, Decker. Now, I'm sure you're not a good boy. Am I right?"

"Uh, yeah." He flicked his gaze away and down.

Guilty. Excellent.

"Anything you've ever done that's particularly bad?"

"Like, sexually?"

Good grief. These men thought about nothing else with an attractive woman in front of them. That single-mindedness in her prey was why she excelled at her job, why her disguise helped her accomplish her goals. The possibility of sex worked every time. So predictable, these men.

If not for the need to stay ahead of her quota of kills, she'd have walked away and tried again tomorrow night. This man was that disgusting. But this criminal would do for her knife's needs.

Twirling a long, flaxen strand of hair around her finger, she giggled. "Oh, Decker, I'm sure you're into all kinds of kink. But what I'm talking about is other naughty things. You ever been in jail? Or maybe should've been in jail?"

He snorted. "You the police?"

"Not even close. I like bad boys. They turn me on."

He put his hand on the wall on the other side of her head and pressed his groin into hers. She resisted the urge to curl her lip and kick him in that offensive yet small bulge. Even though she might enjoy playing the temptress, she was never tempted, especially by a guy like this.

"What do you want to know?" His chest rose and fell more quickly now.

She batted her eyes. "Tell me the worst thing you've ever done in your entire life."

"You don't want to hear it, babe."

Babe. Seriously. "Oh, yes I do. It turns me on—"

She froze.

What was that? A brief flicker of movement high on a nearby building distracted her. Seeing nothing, she dragged her attention back to the balding biker.

"Well, once I ..."

His stale cigarette breath offended as he put his lips to her ear and whispered the sin. Or sins.

The hot air crawled over her neck as he spoke. "... and she might have been fifteen years old, but she acted eighteen. I mean, how was I supposed to know? But her mother, now that lady was tasty ..."

The knife throbbed, hungry, as her intense need to consume criminal blood escalated. Repugnant didn't even begin to describe this monster. What a delicious feast for the knife.

It might even qualify for the Meaningful Kill, the one act that could release her from the eternal, hated contract. A girl could hope.

As an Indebted, her boss was Satan in human form, Jerahmeel. Such a nasty, horrifying creature. Her life had boiled down to killing felons to feed Jerahmeel's appetite for the evil amassed in these sinners.

How she would love to be done with this hellish quasi-existence, to be done with disguises and hiding. And was it asking too much to ask to be left alone?

To do what? Rot? Beyond her ever-present duty to kill criminals and her mundane job as personal attendant for Barnaby, an ex-Indebted, she had nothing. No purpose.

She shoved the thought out of her mind and focused on the creep in front of her.

The minute his tongue touched her earlobe, she shoved him away, spun him around, and slammed him into the wall.

"Let me verify what you've told me," she said.

"What the hell?" He struggled against her supernaturally strong grip.

She dug her fingers into his arm, not caring how badly it hurt. Glancing around, she prayed Jerahmeel wouldn't take this opportunity to pop in. Jerahmeel fixated on people with extra powers, and he already had too keen of an interest in her—a bad combination. If he found out about her additional mind-reading skill, her life would be a living hell. Actually, her life already was a living hell. It would simply become worse than now. Hard to imagine.

Pay attention. Get this job done and get out.

With one more quick glance to ensure no one approached, she steadied the biker's goateed chin, entered his consciousness, and did something no creature alive today—human or otherwise — knew she could do. She *pulled* the thoughts from his mind.

Digging past the mental curtains where he thought about sex and beer, she pushed deeper into the glowing ember of his crime. His horror at the inner invasion coated her own thoughts like cold, wet cobwebs. She mentally gripped the image of his crime and dragged it into her own consciousness, while adjusting his perception to reduce his sweaty panic. Good. Now he believed that her exploration of his mind was all part of fabulous foreplay.

"That's nice, babe," he murmured, trapped in her thrall.

Forcing a smile, she held him in place as she teased out the details. A few years ago, he had done horrible, unspeakable things. Brutal, drawn-out, bloody torture. His glistening, red hand on the ankle of—oh God, a child. A tiny figure hung from ropes that bit into thin, bruised arms. The grisly images flooding her mind wrenched at her stomach.

This man would suit the knife's need for a corrupt and tasty soul, to say nothing of her kick-ass alter ego's desire to deliver vengeance against everything evil. She hated confirming the crimes because of the after-images that remained imprinted on her memories, but her hidden talent was another way she could assert some control over her despised existence as an Indebted killer.

Of course, the knife signaled which criminal to kill, so why bother using her power?

An overabundance of caution, even after all these years. If she accidentally murdered an innocent, she might lose what sanity she had left. So she double-checked her kill. Every single time.

Also, if she picked only the worst sinners, maybe she'd increase her chances of obtaining the Meaningful Kill. Besides, she needed to flog her conscience with the horrible images of the criminals' deeds, to serve small penance for deserting her own children so many years ago when she became this Indebted killer.

Truth be told, she also enjoyed each small burst of vigilante retribution, bringing the crimes to light. Right before committing a crime herself. Because warped logic was better than no logic.

She shoved him harder into the wall. The idiot thought they were headed for wild sex.

"Oh yeah, baby. You like it rough?" He fumbled with his belt buckle.

You've got to be kidding. "You have no idea," she whispered. "Let me get some protection."

She bent down and reached for the knife, which rested in the sheath on her lower leg. Her night had gone from routine quota kill to an all-consuming need to kill in the space of mere seconds. Damned Indebted hunger drove her into a frenzy, despite her typical control.

"Yeah, do it, baby."

Another movement from the rooftop, like a moth passing in front of a light, stole her attention for a split second.

The movement distracted her. At the moment her fingers grasped the handle, Decker kicked her square in the chest. Despite fast reflexes, she didn't react in time and bent over, coughing. The knife clattered a few feet away, next to Decker. The blade glowed lurid green, hungry. Damn, it physically hurt not to touch her knife.

Thankfully, the damaged muscles and cracked ribs had already begun to knit back together.

"You gonna pull that shit on me?"

She edged toward the blade. Had to reconnect with it. Needed it. Now.

He followed her gaze. "You want this?" He kicked the knife into the depths of the courtyard. Then he pulled a gun from a side holster.

She crouched, ready to bolt over and retrieve her weapon. Longing for the blade threatened to drive her mad.

Before she could act, a dark figure landed in front of her with a heavy thud of boots on cobblestones and a long trench coat flapping around him, making him appear too large for life.

What in the blazes?

"Step away from the lady, *mon ami*."

"Who the fuck are you?" Decker sneered, pointing the gun at the man in black.

"Someone you don't want to cross." The man's voice, a rich tenor with a Cajun lilt, cut through the evening air. Although his voice held lightness, almost humor, he commanded attention, not by his giant frame looming out of the shadows but by a tantalizing charisma when he spoke.

No time to ponder how his voice slid over her like a satin sheet. She needed to get rid of this extra Musketeer, fast. Bless this hapless hero, but she was most certainly *not* a damsel in distress. Quite the opposite, and she was managing fine before he arrived. Now, if only he would leave her alone to complete her assignment. Then she could wrap this job up and go back to being inconspicuous.

"Get the fuck out of here!" Decker screamed as the gun shook.

When the man in the trench coat didn't move, the biker pulled the trigger.

The mystery guy moved faster than her eye could follow. The gunshot crack echoed through the courtyard. The sound was sure to draw attention. Not good.

Even though he rocked back a step, the unfortunate gallant remained standing.

No.

Still standing.

He brushed a hand over his chest, like a gnat had bit him.

She ducked into the shadows of the courtyard, found her knife, shoved it in the holster, and raced back. She had to get rid of hero-boy so her biker buddy could feed the blade.

With a gurgled grunt and wheeze, Decker crumpled to the ground.

What in the hell?

The large man stood over Decker's body as a pool of dark liquid stained the cobblestones beneath his feet. Soul's blood, wasted.

God, she had needed to let her knife drink that criminal's blood. Now her compulsion to kill had doubled, threatening to blind her. Ignoring the man, she knelt next to the dead biker. She took a deep breath, fought searing pain in her gut due to her missed kill, and wrestled her base desires back under control. Damn, citizens would be here soon. She had to move.

Was that green glint in the interloper's hand a trick of the light? With her knife lust, she couldn't trust her perception of reality. His weapon looked suspiciously like ... hers. That meant he was ... oh, hell.

If he didn't yet realize that they were both Indebted, it might give her a brief advantage.

Oh God, what if this was Barnaby's friend they'd come to visit? Surely not. How many Indebted could inhabit New Orleans without drawing attention? Several, right? New Orleans was a big city.

The would-be rescuer held out a hand, and despite her best judgment, she took it, noting his broad fingers and a hint of dark hair on the back of his wrist. She needed to get out of here, but something about him fascinated her. Another Indebted. How old was he?

With a wince, he drew her up in front of him. The small hole in his coat spoke to the gunshot wound beneath. The injury probably hurt like hell but would be well on its way to healing.

Standing in front of him now, her gaze rested right on his shadowed mouth, where she could make out a smirk of sensual lips. For a split second, she wondered what those lips would feel like on hers. Would they be warm and sensual or demanding and hard? Would they stay turned up at the corners?

Was he actually smiling like this ridiculous situation was some joke? She withdrew her hand from his heated grip and clamped down on her girlish thoughts. One hundred and fifty years old, and all of a sudden she felt flirty? Incredible ... and incredibly inappropriate.

"Why the hell did you do that?" She gestured toward the hemorrhaging biker.

Although the Indebted's face was mostly hidden in shadow, his one visible eye widened and he reared back. Dark hair curled beneath his fedora—were those strands as soft as they appeared? He rubbed the hair on his chin, less than a full beard but more than stubble. The scratchy sound sent a quiver of desire into her belly. While the knife pulsed with sick hunger on her leg, she itched with longing to touch the rough hair on the man's jaw.

"I don't understand. That man would have killed you," he said.

"I can take care of myself, thanks." She needed to feed the blade. Soon.

Voices drifted down the street, getting louder by the second. Damn it.

"*Pardonnez?*" His jaw dropped open, and the dark gaze bored into her. No, *through* her. She shivered.

"You ruined my evening." Probably not the most typical human response. After all, she'd just witnessed him murder a man. Sadly, though, she had become pretty blasé about the job requirements. Dead was dead.

Shaking with the effort to restrain the drive to kill, she clenched her hands into fists. The knife wanted her to wrap her fingers around the hilt and plunge the blade into a chest. Her hunger had risen to such a level, it would feed on anyone, including innocents and even her own kind. But this errant knight in proverbial shining armor shouldn't suffer because of her inability to focus.

She curbed her killing desires, just like she regulated other aspects of her life. Well, the areas she *could* control, that is.

With her efforts, the knife lust slowly ebbed. Sad emptiness took its place.

"You're ... unhappy that I saved you?" He grimaced, revealing square, even teeth.

"You wouldn't understand."

"Try me."

His mellow voice soothed her raw nerves like aloe on a wound. When he stepped forward, she jerked backward. Time to get away from this guy and from this scene, fast.

Shouts drifted into the courtyard. Citizens would be here in a matter of seconds.

"Sir, thank you for your help, however misguided. I need to be on my way."

"Thank you? That's it?" He gestured at Decker's body, motionless and silent in the cool night.

At the wry undertone, she pressed her lips together. Was he making fun of her?

Anger bubbled up. What did it say about her own humanity that the corpse at her feet disappointed her? Pissed her off. Not because he was dead, but because she hadn't been the one to kill him.

Here she stood in her ridiculous wig and urban fantasy getup, using sex to draw in her prey, like a warped black widow. For what?

Somewhere deep down, she wasn't this seductress, despite her fabulous disguise. All the air and energy left her in a rush. All bravado, no substance. She was a fraud, living in a shell of an existence.

Damn, how she wanted Decker's criminal blood inside of her knife. What if she just swirled the knife in the pool of cold blood? Maybe that would work.

No, it wouldn't. Had to be blood from the heart; the knife had to be in the chest. Damn it.

"Thank you. Goodnight, sir," she said in her firmest tone.

He stepped close enough that she saw his closely trimmed facial hair framing upturned lips, a mouth full enough to give a provocative smirk. A combination of cologne and Cajun spice blended perfectly around him. For a moment, she wanted to indulge, to taste, to experience a different life, to be someone else.

What the hell was wrong with her? With a dead body cooling at her feet, a handsome but still-clueless Indebted before her, and citizens on their way, she fixated on his mouth?

The damn blade pulsed again, again eager for someone's—anyone's—blood. It insisted on her complete attention, pulling her focus away from the man in front of her.

When she tried to evade him, he snagged her arm. He was strong, but of course, she was his equal. He couldn't budge her. At the display of her Indebted strength, shock crossed the visible part of his features. Yes, they shared the exact same secret.

"*Chèri*? What the—?"

Using his surprise to her advantage, she acted on pure instinct, stomping his instep with her spiked heel. He bit off a curse as his grip loosened. Dropping to a crouch, she rotated and swept an outstretched foot under the one leg he hopped on, and he fell hard onto the cobblestones. Unfortunately, when she rotated, her stupid wig caught on his hand, knocking it askew and covering an eye.

Not caring if he saw, she tugged her hair back in place. In one fluid motion, she leapt to the metal fire escape ladder and vaulted to a roof. Quite a feat in heels. How did those sexy vampire chicks in the novels manage? Never mind. No time to think about silly books.

She gritted her teeth and sprinted across the roof. Before descending the next ladder to the opposite street, she glanced back into the courtyard. She had gotten away in the nick of time. Patrons from the bar rounded the corner into the courtyard, followed by a police officer.

Decker's body was gone, a glistening puddle on the cobblestones all that remained.

The mystery man, too, was gone. Although he wasn't actually a mortal man but Indebted. Just like her.

He must have removed the body.

Why?

To protect her.

To take attention away from things in this world that could not be explained.

What a joke. Her entire existence couldn't be explained. Everything she did as a result of being Indebted defied logic. How would a dead criminal change that fact?

It wouldn't.

But a pattern of dead criminals could bring unwanted scrutiny to the Indebted that called New Orleans their home. Where had her consideration for others gone?

To hell, along with the greater portion of her conscience.

Jumping from the roof to adjacent buildings, she continued to the end of the block. There was no easy fire escape. She peered down the four story building and sighed. This was going to hurt.

She dropped off the roof, landing with an audible pop on one foot. A red wave of pain swamped her, and she gripped the edge of the brick to clear her head. Masonry disintegrated under her fingertips.

She pressed her lips together to keep from crying out.

Breathe.

Another few seconds, and she'd be functional.

With another crunch, her bones knitted back together enough for her to walk. Each step felt better than the last.

Once she reached the French District, she ducked into a dark corner behind a dumpster and pressed her fingers to her forehead. So tired. In the past, she had salvaged botched kills, but tonight was different. She still needed to kill, but the control she had exerted over that biker's mind took so much energy. Her fatigue would keep the desire to kill in check for a short period of time. The desperation no longer consumed her.

Sick consolation. For now.

Meeting a fellow Indebted had thrown her for a loop. True, some Indebted worked together, but Ruth operated in private, always had. She hated spectators of any kind. Ironic, then, how she'd given the man in the trench coat quite a show.

Like most of her kind, she avoided hunting in the daytime. More potential witnesses. So she would have to endure a miserable day until tomorrow night. Even though time technically meant nothing to her, twenty-four hours from now seemed like years away.

Maybe as a diversion she could indulge in a tiny fantasy about her hero's sensual lips.

Don't miss the other exciting books in Jillian David's Hell to Pay series:

Relentless Flame
"The sex is hot and steamy while not being gratuitous or overbearing. I love the characters she has created, the way they support each other and feel like people I would enjoy getting to know. As an independent reviewer for paranormal books and authors that rock, I give this four firm solid and sharp fangs." —*Paranormal Romance and Authors that Rock*, 4 fangs

"Dante's journey from player to genuinely caring man is amusing to watch, since Hannah does not play any kind of game he is used to, and the relationship is worth all their pain." — *InD'Tale Magazi*ne, 4.5 stars

Immortal Flame
"Cleverly and expertly woven between their POVs, their journey is not an easy one - lives will be lost, family endangered, much bodily harm done to many - and love begins to bloom despite neither really wanting it...(T)his series will be an exciting one and well worth the time to savor strength in men, and women." 4.5 Stars — *InD'Tale Magazine*

"Immortal Flame teases and taunts from the beginning, slowly building characters by revealing pieces of their lives and past in bits....Immortal Flame is a slow burn to a fiery furnace..." 5 Stars —*Paranormal Romance Guild*

"Intense and entertaining throughout, Immortal Flame proves a strong start to a promising new series that should prove a treat for fans of this ever popular genre. One to add to your reading list, it is strongly recommended." —*Book Viral*

"A fast-paced and fun paranormal romance. This was a new author for me but one that I will definitely look to read again." —*Night Owl Romance*

"Packed with scorching love scenes, a bit of mystery and plenty of action, Jillian David keeps you wanting more from the very beginning." —Eat Sleep Read Reviews

In the mood for more Crimson Romance?
Check out *Unstoppable by Lynn Crandall*
at *CrimsonRomance.com.*

Printed in the United States
By Bookmasters